# THE OPHIDIAN HORDE

## RYAN SCHOW

River City Publishing

# COPYRIGHT

**THE OPHIDIAN HORDE**

Cover Design by Milo at Deranged Doctor Design

Visit the Author's Website: www.RyanSchow.com

# FOREWORD

I was never a Pinterest person, but my wife is and she was on it enough for me to grow curious. When I got my own page, I found a crazy amount of inspiration for both the stories and the characters within them. I never wanted to keep this to myself, so I started a Pinterest board for every book in this series. These inspirational pictures include character photos, the cars and the places where my characters reside. If you're signed up for Pinterest (which is easy and free!) then visit me at: **https:// www.pinterest.com/ryanschowwriter/boards/**. Also, if you haven't joined The Last War's Private Facebook Group, please click over there now as I love to chat with readers regularly as well as post cool inspirational pictures, some of the real life stories that inspired this series, cover reveals for the new books and sample chapters of books before they come out. You can request to join this private group by typing THE LAST WAR FAN GROUP in the Facebook browser (search bar). I'll see you there!

# CHAPTER ONE

When my brother Rex announced that the flash in the sky could very well be the result of a nuclear EMP counter-strike, Macy wanted to know if the toilets would still flush. I'm worried about the end of the world; she's worried about where all the poop will go.

Naturally, Rex said *no*. He said the toilets wouldn't flush.

He couldn't say, *we'll see*, or *maybe*. It was a definite and resounding *no*. As if he hadn't a thought in his mind about scaring my daughter, his niece.

I open my mouth to tell him to have some common sense, but Macy is already speaking so the rush of words dies in the back of my throat instead.

"Well whomever invented sewers and toilets was a genius," Macy says. "I mean, can you imagine having to dig a hole in the back yard every time you have to...do your thing?"

"Macy!" I say, stifling a laugh.

She looks at me, but Rex is already laughing, which I'm afraid might encourage her further and this has me firing him a look. It doesn't matter, though. I take in all of us, with our dirty hair and our filthy clothes, and I think, *thank God the toxic rain has stopped!*

And if Rex is right about the EMP, then that would mean that perhaps the drones have stopped, too.

He says that was the point.

The clouds are still a leaden grey, the sky a wash of slow moving smoke. Even the air stinks of burnt things and people, which makes me wonder how many more rains we'll need before this city is finally scrubbed clean of this nightmare.

"Before the dawn of civilization, you just dropped your britches and went where you needed to," Rex says, keeping the issue alive like some sort of spastic teenager. "When you're done, you just kick a little dirt over it and bingo, you're done. It'll probably be like that now that the power's out."

I wonder if having just been shot and held hostage in the field has turned his brain upside down. What is wrong with him?

"Will you two please stop," I ask, flashing Macy warning eyes. Then to my brother, it's a hard stare followed by, "You should know better."

"Lighten up, Cincinnati, we've just survived a traumatic experience."

"This whole last month has been a traumatic experience."

He shrugs his good arm and shows me a smirk that says he'll try to behave, but only to appease me. At this point, the fact that he's not showing pain is pretty amazing, especially considering our mad dash from downtown to the Presidio left our friend Gunner dead and Rex shot in the arm.

"These are questions critical to our survival," Macy argues, totally serious. "Especially when you have to go number two. I mean think about it—"

"I have been," I argue.

"What about when we run out of toilet paper? Are we supposed to just paw ourselves clean with our hands? Or should we use old copies of the Wall Street Journal? Or whatever socks have the biggest holes in them?"

"That's gross," I say.

"Well if Uncle Rex is saying this is basically the end of the world," Macy continues, undeterred, "then these are serious questions in need of honest answers."

"There's also the garbage to consider," Stanton says, chiming in. "Humans are good at making waste. A lot of it."

"Can you please not add to this?" I ask, leveling him with a stare.

I'm starting to feel outnumbered here.

"You'll find what you need for now," Indigo says over her shoulder, "and we'll figure out the rest as we go. Think of this as a journey, not a destination."

By now we're following this mysterious teen down Jackson Street and I'm not exactly sure where we're going, only that this tall, skinny thing told us we're heading to the Panhandle at the edge of Golden Gate Park, which feels like forever away.

Without meaning to, I begin to wonder what in God's name turned this poor girl into this hunter/killer before us. I want to know who she is, how she came to be where she was the minute we needed her, what she's hoping to get out of helping us.

Trudging through this apocalyptic nightmare, the air growing damp again, but the smoke clearing somewhat, I can't help but shiver. It's not the cold, it's this place. It's eerie. Haunting. Like some sort of weighted stillness has fallen over the streets. The same ghostly silence that settles over a battlefield after the cowards and the weak have fled and the last warrior has fallen. Somewhere a woman is sobbing. All around us, desperate souls wander the streets, not sure where to go, what to do, how to cope with this awful new future.

I don't blame them.

To my husband (who's doing his best to keep up despite the gash he received on the back of his head from when our apartment was raided by thugs pretending to be cops), I move near him, lower my voice and say, "These people out here are...they're just...they're aimless, vacant, afraid. Is that us? Are we those people, too, but we just don't know it yet?"

He looks at me and gives a slow nod that lets me know he

understands exactly what I'm saying, and exactly what's on my mind.

"Our daughter killed a man," he whispers. He says it so low I practically have to read his lips to truly get the message. Beneath my breast, a rolling ache starts up again.

"How's your head?" I ask, changing the subject.

There's no mention of what I did to save him back at our house, the man I shot point blank, how all of us almost died in the apartment we stole from a defenseless old lady who ended up dead and stashed on a hillside because of us.

Touching the tender spot on the back of his head, he doesn't make the face I expect. The slightest little surprised expression brightens his features instead. "If I were languishing for attention, I'd say it hurts. But I'm not. Even though it does."

A smile curls my lips despite the emotions grating through me. "If that's the case, you're doing one hell of a job not showing it."

"It's like a scraped knee," he replies, "but on my head."

A small, sad laugh escapes me.

"It's a bit more than that," I say, knowing the wound will need to be cleaned and stitched up. "But I'm glad you're okay."

I turn back to the road ahead, to the graveyard of houses and businesses, to the abandoned cars and the bodies both alive and dead, and I think to myself, how will I stitch up his cut with no medical equipment?

*One tragedy at a time, Sin...*

Bone tired and weary, our little group tramps along a dozen more blocks, working to keep up with Indigo. We walk past rack and ruin; we walk past a thousand destroyed dreams; we walk past endless proof that the future I once imagined now rests on a different timeline in a different universe that will be nothing like this one we see before us.

More than once I make eye contact with people wandering by. My heart feels destroyed with every interaction. It's like looking into deep space and hoping to find life, but seeing only vast emptiness instead. Some of these walking corpses want water, or our help; some just sit there on the curbs and cry out loud or weep quietly to themselves; some have their eyes open and it's abundantly clear that no one is home, that no one will ever be home again.

By now an hour of walking has passed. My feet ache but I won't say it. I want to scream, to cry, to let this thunderous well of grief break loose in the mother of all explosions, but my time in the ER taught me many things, one of which is to break down on your own time, away from the action, far from the eyes of your peers and patients.

So I follow Indigo almost aimlessly, feeling the light dying in my eyes, cataloguing the ever increasing drain this new burden is putting upon my body, my mind and my soul.

"Look at these people," I hear myself saying to no one in general.

"Zombies," Indigo says.

Not real zombies. Just people on their way to nowhere. Stumbling towards a future that existed in the past only to realize the years ahead are a now a God-sized blank slate. A blank slate dusted with the ash of a civilization that's been burned to the ground in a matter of weeks presumably by terrors of their own creation.

If these zombies are anything like me, then perhaps they're wondering what will happen next. Will we starve to death? Get killed by more of those Ophidian psychos? Trust a stranger with our lives, our well being, our future only to be left weak and vulnerable?

The future is uncertain. It's an empty ocean. A million miles of sand without a picture of what to expect, what to hope for, how to live.

"Rex?" I hear myself asking.

He looks back at me and I almost don't know what to say. Perhaps this is a part of me reaching to the man I know will protect us.

"Yeah?" he asks, keeping pace with Indigo. He sees the panic in my eyes, but I put it away fast, not realizing it was trying to get out.

"Are you okay?" I ask. "Your head and your arm, I mean."

When our helicopter ride out of town left us behind only to crash seconds later, Rex went down hard and was taken hostage by a pack of savages. At the time he was dealing with a gunshot wound to his arm. The gangbangers in the field thought they could get his compliance by cracking him over the head with a rifle. It was a temporary solution to a problem they didn't know they had: us.

"If you're thinking we're in dire straights, big sis, we are. But I've survived worse, and I can tell you this: we'll be okay, even if it doesn't feel like it."

"Says the guy who got scratched by a bullet and passed out," I joke.

"What can I say?" he replies with a grin. "I'm a terrible victim."

He says this like we're on some grand Disneyland adventure as opposed to the real life set of *Terminator Meets Escape From New York,* but in San Francisco. If this were Disneyland, we'd call the ride, "A Trip Through The Apocalypse" and the background music would be harsh and foreboding, and most certainly scored by Nine Inch Nails.

Rex follows up with: "You have that look on your face like you're wanting to take charge, but don't know how."

My mouth opens, but nothing comes out. He knows he's right. Smiling—casual like it's coffee shop conversation—he returns his eyes and his focus to the road ahead.

I'm reeling by his complete dismissal, but this isn't my thing. Survival. I'm strong, but not a born leader. I'm tough and resilient and determined to protect my family at all costs, but I can't fight, except to shoot one gun reasonably well.

There's this huge part of me still trying to shoulder back the memories of what just happened: the drones, Gunner's death, the attack in the field, the EMP...

Everything is replaying in my head. All of it. Just piling on one tragedy after another. For a second, it's so crippling I find myself falling behind the pack.

When we lost our helicopter ride out of this hellhole and came face to face with some of this city's more nightmarish residents—scumbags we killed trying not to die or be taken prisoner —the reality of this bitter new existence set in and I got scared. I *am* scared. Scared for Macy, for Stanton and Rex, for me...

Even now, the thought of finding a new home, gathering up our things by stealing from others, then defending said home like it's the old west, has my blood curdling. Heightened levels of dread bloom fresh within me, tugging at my resolve, giving me pause.

"You okay?" Stanton says, studying me with concerned eyes. He slows his pace, but I tell him to keep going, that I'm fine even though I'm most certainly not.

If not for the horrors we've already witnessed, many of which we were complicit in, this new world would have broken me by now.

I feel myself cracking.

The memories begin to spin, overlapping each other, blurring the details but piling on the trauma and the chaos. I don't think I can do this.

*But you have to...*

I must.

They took Rex. They almost killed him. Macy and I were just bodies in their eyes. Future slaves. Vessels by which these creatures hoped to sate their darker, more carnal needs.

A cold stab of fear hits me not for what we escaped, but for what could have happened. What did happen was our group stamped out their group thanks to Indigo, Rex and Macy.

*Oh God, Macy.*

The one thing I've been so afraid of has come true. Am I the only one affected by this? Looking at Stanton, who seems to be pushing on without much emotion, and certainly not one single complaint, I get so mad at him. He knows, though.

He feels it, too.

He sees our future changing, slipping away. He sees how this world might eventually turn our daughter into a monster, or worse, a statistic.

He's just doing the best he can, I tell myself.

Same as me.

Across the street, which is littered with abandoned cars, a man is trying to kick down a door. Up ahead, a wife is beating on her husband's shoulder, yelling at him in what sounds like Russian, but he's somewhere else, ignoring her, just staring straight ahead like there's nothing in his head but dead space.

Two dogs are running up on us: a pair of brindle-colored pugs with their leashes dragging behind them. We all step out of the way and they hustle by, snorting and panting, and obviously moving toward something with some sort of mystery purpose.

When we come upon the woman beating her husband, she's fallen to her knees and is sobbing, and he's just standing there, looking down at her, not sure how to help her.

Hard times make for some damn hard choices, and these times are so trying, so difficult, so terrifying it's hard to think we have anything left *but* hard choices. I'm not even sure I'm equipped to live this kind of life. Will I end up like the woman we just passed? Breaking down on Stanton after this life has beaten and bested us? The big problem here isn't us, though. It's not even my daughter doing what she did or becoming the monster our young friend Indigo just might be. The problem is that in a pinch, I failed to act as decisively as Indigo did.

You hesitate, you're dead.

Truth.

Will I die? Here I am, swallowed in fear, lamenting the loss of Macy's innocence, wondering if I have what it takes to survive and Macy's up ahead talking with Rex about a life without *The Kardashians.*

Seeing her taking the end of the world in stride, I shake loose these toxic thoughts and push forward, realizing I can't hang behind or I'll drag everyone else back with me. I want to be closer to my baby, my brother. Stanton.

"A life without the Kardashians would be a peaceful world," Indigo chimes in, expecting a quick response but getting a confused stare from Macy instead.

"Well I like them," Macy says, a little breathless.

"So it seems," Indigo replies.

"You don't?"

"Name one thing they ever did that added to the community, to mankind or to the furthering of a society of impressionable young women looking for a role model," Indigo challenges almost without expression.

"For starters," Macy says, "they made it okay to have a big butt."

Up ahead, I see a smile slowly creep onto Indigo's face. Macy watches for the response, then grins when she sees the archer's face light up.

"Yeah," Rex says, "I'm going to miss the Kardashians, too."

"Shut up, Rex," I say, and everyone starts to laugh.

Then Rex halfway busts out with the lyrics of a famous Sir Mix A Lot tune: "I like big butts and I cannot lie..." and that brittle edge of hopelessness no longer feels so cutting. It's a swift moment that's sure to pass, but for now, I revel in it.

My gaze jumps from Macy to Rex to Stanton, and then it slides back to Indigo. Here we are, in the middle of hell on earth, surrounded by loved ones and an uncanny savior, and I can't stop marveling at how swiftly we're moving into the fierce unknown.

We don't have anything right now but each other for strength and our determination to live. But with all of us smiling and Rex's odd sense of humor to thank for that, the more hopeful side of me thinks it might just be enough.

# CHAPTER TWO

Rex seems to have some sort of crush on Indigo. Macy's talking to Rex, but Rex is looking at Indigo and Indigo isn't paying attention to either of them. Knowing Rex, any moment now he's going to find a way to tell his latest conquest one or more of his war stories.

The truth about my brother isn't as glamorous as the tall tales of his escapades in the sand. In Afghanistan, Rex was taken hostage for what I gather was somewhere between a week and a month before he was rescued. He won't tell me how long it actually was, but with what he survived, I wonder if he even knows how long he was in there.

After he was rescued, Rex spent a little over two weeks in a triage center trying not to die. Many men would come back from Afghanistan changed, broken even, but not my little brother. The second Rex was discharged from the hospital, he went right back to the war.

When I asked why he did this, he told me he was going to have to leave the war behind one way or another. Best to leave having fought rather than leave it as a beaten man who almost died. In a screwy sort of way, I understand this. How for him this rationale made perfect sense.

As much as he never talks about the details of his capture, not with me and certainly not in the company of other girls, Rex has this amazing ability to weave some high lies into some believable truths. He's so convincing. So animated.

All this just to hook up with strangers.

When I confronted him about his "philanthropic ways," he told me he was simply turning lemons into lemonade. He was dating a blonde high school girl who was eighteen by a day back then.

"What will you tell her parents when she misses her period?" I remember asking. I was really bothered back then because even though he hadn't changed much outwardly, he had definitely changed.

That was the first and last time we ever conversed on the subject of responsibility concerning the opposite sex. Glancing over at Indigo, though—if it should come to that—I'm pretty sure I'll drag the subject up again and stay with it until I feel better, which might be never.

On the bright side, and much to my delight, not every girl falls for Rex's lofty narratives, his interesting sense of humor or his charm. And thank God. I almost lost him to the middle east; I'm not quite ready to lose him to girl.

Then along comes Indigo...

Someone who's vastly different from my brother's little cadre of youngsters.

Will my little brother's charm work on someone like her? Looking at this young woman, measuring her obvious disinterest in him, her incredible focus on the road ahead, I'd venture to say probably not. The kind of girls who fall for Rex are always checking their hair, their lipstick, their teeth. Indigo seems like she'd rather shoot someone than fix her hair.

Fortunately for all of us, Rex's eyes remain focused on the road ahead, and he says nothing about his military exploits. This has me studying Indigo. For some strange reason, I think I'm enamored by the girl.

No, I'm sure of it.

Staring at the back of her head, I wonder, *what is it that drives her?* There's something dark and ferocious propelling her forward. Even when she's standing still, behind her eyes she looks like she's charging forward, ready to pulverize anything or anyone in her way.

I shake my head, look away, try to think of something else. My stomach rumbles, causing me to slow my pace again, but only for a second. No need reminding everyone we have nothing to eat, no place to live, and no backyards for which to dig holes we'll later call toilets.

I want to say something to Stanton, or Rex. Discuss our grim situation hoping one of them might be able to chase away some of my mounting anxieties, but first things first: we need someplace to call home. Indigo offered to help, so we're taking her up on it. If we can solve this one problem first, then all the other little problems might seem a bit more manageable. Certainly not so overwhelming.

*One thing at a time, Sin,* I remind myself yet again.

Indigo finally turns and looks at Rex, who sees this and gives her one of his trademark grins; her response is a decisive frown.

"Stop looking at me like that," she says. That smile falls right off his face, making me grin inside. "I need to ask you a serious question."

"Okay..."

"I need your help," she tells him.

At this point I'm eavesdropping, trying to close the distance between us, but not enough to reveal my intentions.

"I'm listening," Rex says.

"I've been watching these guys for a few days," she tells him.

"The guys that attacked us? The ones you shot?"

"The one that got away, back in the field? I'm fairly certain he'll have headed back to their little gangbanger's squatter palace. Which is a Walgreen's if you can imagine. We need to get to him, interrogate him. See if there are more of them. You seem to have a tolerance for this sort of thing—"

"What sort of thing?"

"War."

Smiling, he says, "Ah, yes."

"You a soldier?"

"Did a few tours, but I'm retired for now."

"You're too young to be retired."

"We're all retired," he says. "Seriously, look around. The daily grind isn't about punching a clock as much as it's about not getting our clocks punched."

Her mouth twitches and I can tell he thinks he's said something clever.

"Can you fight or not?" she asks.

"That's a silly question," he replies, deadpan, his eyes fixed on her.

"Sure it's not, *soldier*," she quips, returning to her confident, purposeful, isolated walk. "Just know things are about to get a little bloody."

"Bloody for whom?"

"Not us if we play our cards right," she says, not meeting his eyes.

Hearing this conversation between them, I'm starting to wonder if she's got a handle on things, or if she's about to get us into the kind of trouble we were fortunate enough to have just escaped.

"How'd you find us in the first place?" Rex asks.

"I wasn't looking," she says.

Rex's got his eyes on a pack of travelers ahead of us, moving quickly. There's another guy across the street on all fours in the gutter throwing up. Some pre-teen girl is sitting on the curb a few feet from him with a dirty Teddy Bear tucked in her armpit. She's picking her teeth.

"You weren't looking, yet you found us anyway," Rex replies.

"Lucky me."

Rex now turns and glares at her.

"I told you I've been tracking these guys," she finally admits.

"Why?"

She gives him *the look*. "If you'll let me finish? Please? My God, you're like a dog with a hard-on. And not terribly bright."

He frowns and says, "Well your communication skills suck."

"I get that."

"What did they do to you to turn you into...*this?*" he asks, motioning to the whole of her.

"And suddenly he's a little smarter than he looks."

The jab makes me smile. Yeah, I definitely like this girl. I like that she's keeping Rex on his toes, even though I'm not exactly sure I like where her head is at.

"Vigilantes never start out as vigilantes," he says. "They're made."

"Is that how you see me?"

"You put an arrow in the guy's head from fifty yards out."

"My grandpa taught me to shoot."

"Congratulations?"

Indigo shakes her head, and I have half a mind to smack my little brother, but he's a grown man, perfectly capable of making his own choices and mistakes if he wants. Looking away, almost like she's somewhere else, like she's trying to decide how to say it, she finally says, "Those cretins did the unthinkable."

Everything about my brother changes: his demeanor, how tall he's standing, the way he's looking at her—everything...it's just...*different.*

If Rex is anything like me, we're both wondering what could be so bad that she resorted to tracking these guys down and killing them with neither reluctance nor mercy.

"I spent a lot of time in the middle east," Rex says. "Not to sound like one of those jack hounds who's always trying to one-up everyone, but what you call unthinkable here is very different from the unthinkable there."

"Well I wasn't in the middle east, but bad is bad and what these guys are about to do is worse than bad. I can feel it."

In a rare moment of kindness, or compassion rather, Rex softens his eyes and says, "I'm sorry, Indigo. For whatever happened to you."

Indigo doesn't say anything for a few blocks, not until Macy asks how much longer.

"Rex an I need to grab a few things at the Walgreens on the corner of 22$^{nd}$ and Irving," Indigo tells her, "and from there it's only a few blocks more."

I have a feeling that what Indigo plans on grabbing are the balls and throats of these creeps who seem to possess very little regard for the lives of innocents.

"Please tell me there's food there," Macy replies, "because my stomach is currently digesting itself."

"I think there's food there," she answers. Then: "Maybe even a few rolls of toilet paper."

"Perhaps we could find a shovel, too," Rex says. "That way we can dig a toilet wherever we land."

She looks at him, not a trace of humor in her lovely eyes, and says, "This isn't a joke."

"I've been in the thick of it before, Indigo."

"Is that supposed to encourage me?"

"This is home. Not some hellhole overseas. The landscape and our enemies are different, but in the end, war is war. You have to be flexible. Which I am. And you can't think long term, not while you're up to your tits in it, which I'm not."

"Cute," she says, while I'm just shaking my head.

"Long term is fifteen minutes from now," he continues, undeterred. "Me? I'm on a minute-by-minute basis. That's all about to change, though. On the off chance that you haven't noticed, the only reason we're able to walk around out in the open without getting blown to smithereens is because that explosion in the sky was an EMP that wiped out the drones."

"You think?" she says.

"Listen," he tells her. "What do you hear?"

She listens. We all listen. Where we're at, the only sounds we hear are our own footfalls on the asphalt.

"EMP," Rex says again.

"Electromagnetic Pulse," Indigo replies.

"As of this moment, we've got a different set of problems we can't fix right away."

"Such as?"

"Food, water, shelter."

"Not a problem just yet," Indigo says, confident. "What else?"

"Ummmmm, we've just been blown back to the stone age, in case you haven't figured it out."

"I'm young, but not naïve."

"Perfect."

"Before we worry about that, we've got to clean up these problems. Which is why we're going to the Walgreen's. The point is, I need to know you have my back."

He snorts out a hearty laugh, then says, "Of course I've got your six." She looks at him, somber. He gives her a steadfast nod. Then: "Look, you saved our collective bacon back there, so I'm happy to return the favor."

"We may have to kill some bad people," she says, her voice low, like she's trying to hide it from Macy.

"Didn't we already have this conversation?" he asks with a cocky grin.

"We're not killing anyone," I hiss at them.

"Stay out of this, Sin," Rex says.

Behind me, Macy and Stanton are talking. Not paying attention to any of this...*scheming*.

"Killing people isn't exactly my forte," Indigo finally admits.

"For being green, you certainly look the part," Rex tells her, not looking at her when he says this.

Now it's Indigo's turn to steal a look at Rex. He meets her gaze. She doesn't pull away this time, but he's not smiling either.

"At the Walgreen's," she says, her words bleak, her expression truly grim. "That's where they're at."

"What's your angle?" he asks, lowering his voice even more.

"A Charles Manson style interrogation."

Grinning, he says, "Man, they must've really done a number on you."

"You have no idea," she grumbles.

# CHAPTER THREE

When the Walgreen's was in sight, Indigo pulled everyone aside and said, "Rex and I need to clear the store first, make sure no one is waiting in there for us. Then we'll check for food and supplies."

"We'll all go," Macy told her, eager. "We're stronger together."

"Stealth is sometimes better than brute force, Macy," Rex told his niece. "What we need from you is to watch our backs, make sure once we're inside we're not followed in and trapped. So if anyone looks like they're coming in behind us, stop them."

"How?"

"Fire off a warning shot," Rex said, preparing himself. Then, looking at Macy, he said, "And preferably not at their head. Not unless it's completely necessary."

"What if there are people in there?" Macy asked.

Rex thought about this. He expected people to be in there— had envisioned it ever since Indigo told him there would be blood—but he wasn't sure if he should tell her what he and Indigo were planning. What were they planning?

"We're counting on there being people inside," Indigo said, fessing up.

"Bad people?" Stanton asked.

"We'll see. If they are, though, I'm pretty sure we can handle them. But if there's shooting, and someone other than me or Rex comes rushing out that door, put a bullet right through their heart. Don't think," Indigo said while looking right at Stanton, "just do it."

"We've got your six," Macy said, sounding much older than she was.

His niece was taking all this a bit too casually, Rex thought as he looked at the young blonde. It hadn't hit her yet: the killing, all this death. When it does, all her carefree bravado will crack and she'll most likely need years of counseling.

He'd seen it all too many times before. Nearly went through it himself.

Rex pulled his eyes off Macy and put them on Stanton. Nodding Macy's way, he said, "Don't let her kill anyone else if you can help it."

"Hey!" Macy said.

"This is not a game," he said. His arm throbbed down deep where he'd been shot and a righteous headache had long ago dulled his senses, but these minor ails paled in comparison to what might come next if Indigo was right. "Stanton, you take the point, followed by Cincinnati, and then you, Macy."

Begrudgingly, his niece acquiesced.

"Good."

"You ready?" Indigo asked.

"Yep."

Indigo took point, but not for long. At the store's alcove and glass door entrance—Rex on one side, Indigo ten feet away on the other—he said, "Lose the bow and arrows."

"They'll be fine."

"Not in tight quarters," he whispered, low and serious. They'd both taken a knee and were now glowering at each other. "You try to turn, snag something on something, you could get us killed. I'm not dying for you in a freaking Walgreen's of all places."

"I said I'm fine," she snapped. "You just worry about you and I'll worry about me."

"You're not listening, *little girl*," he hissed. "Take it off, leave it here, or go back to wherever it was you came from and let me handle this."

Railing him with silent daggers made by eyes that were screaming a million hateful things, they had the mother of all stare downs, which lasted for about thirty seconds with neither of them blinking.

Finally she blew out a breath, slipped her bow off her back, shrugged out of the quiver of arrows and stashed them in a small service alley next door at Sun Maxim's Dim Sum To Go.

"If someone takes my gear, I swear to God I'll shoot you myself," she barked in low tones.

"Save it for the fight," he said. Then, looking at her, his eyes dipped to the twelve inch Ka-bar blade on her side. Pointing to it, he said, "You know how to use that?"

"Looks like carefree Rex is gone," she replied, taking note of his change of attitude. This was war, though, and war has a way of turning on you quick if you get it wrong.

"How many men have you taken down with it?" he asked.

Rolling her eyes, she unsnapped the leather sheath, pulled out the blade and tossed it to him. He caught it by the handle, flipped it over and said, "Wow, just like that?"

"Let's not make a big deal of it," she grumbled.

*Fair enough,* he thought.

With that he nodded, then moved in front of the store's doors, pried one open and held it for Indigo. In one hand Rex held his pistol, in the other Indigo's Ka-bar. In front of him, Indigo was armed with two pistols she'd grabbed off the dead scumbags back in the field. He hated saying it, but she looked incredibly sexy just then.

*Not now,* he thought.

As disagreeable as this girl was proving to be, she was also proving to be quite competent. No one was prepared for a war that found its way stateside, certainly not like this, not from our own technology going rogue, if that's what this was. But she was fitting in just fine.

If he was attracted to her before, he was *really* attracted to her now.

*Not now!*

Shaking off these distracting thoughts, he attuned his senses to his surroundings. The inside was hardly recognizable as a store. Most of the shelves had been looted. Displays were knocked over, aisles pushed this way and that, beds and tents everywhere. It all made for some lousy cover. Even worse, there was a distinct smell of urine and pot smoke in the air. Urine he could stomach; pot smoke residue...not so much.

Deeper inside the store, near the back, he heard voices. He held up a fist; Indigo stopped. She was good with directions, he thought. A plus considering Cincinnati tended to hesitate and Macy tended to rush into things. Stanton, on the other hand, was reliable. For a ragtag gang of untrained talent, it was a start.

He made out two men's voices and a woman's. Rex motioned for Indigo to head up one side of the store and to keep her eyes on him. She nodded. He then signaled that they were going to flank the group and she seemed to understand.

As he moved around an end-cap, he saw a middle-aged man in sweat pants and a touristy t-shirt (one size too small) sitting on the floor with his back against the wall. He wore a trucker's cap with the tag still on, but it was pulled over his eyes and he was sleeping. He had no visible ink, except for the two teardrops tattooed below his eyes.

Looking down, Rex almost stepped into a coil of human excrement. Not fresh, but not crispy either. Poo fumes tickled the air. He stepped over the pile, leaving the fecal artwork behind him where he couldn't smell it.

Standing perfectly still, dead quiet, Rex steadied his breath.

When Rex studied the man, he was pretty sure he knew what he was looking at: a misfit of the violent sort. Scarred knuckles weren't always a true tell to a brawler, but more often than not they were.

Creeping forward, Rex snuck up on the sleeping man, knelt down, then with a burst of force, he drove the Ka-bar's mammoth blade in between the man's fourth and fifth rib. They guy jolted awake in time for Rex to palm-strike the blade the rest of the way in. The man's eyes shot wide open and he drew a sharp breath. Rex quickly covered the man's mouth to silence any sound that may escape and give them away. The man's breath held for a second, then he began to deflate like an old balloon losing air.

Death imminent, his head lolled toward Rex, terribly slow. Pain-stricken eyes slid toward him. He tried to focus, but couldn't. There was no vibrancy left. The body drooped against the blade. Feeling the weight of him on the knife, Rex ripped the Ka-bar out, opening up the man's insides, which would most assuredly lead to rapid and permanent organ failure.

Rex stepped over him, quiet as a mouse, and left him there to die.

Moving forward, unobstructed, he crept toward the sound of the voices. He nearly reached the back of the store when he looked over and saw Indigo waiting for him, giving him the "what gives?" signal. He raised the bloody blade and pointed to it. She nodded in understanding, then used two fingers to tell him she had eyes on the targets. After that she held up three fingers. He nodded. Three subs, confirmed.

She moved forward; he intended to follow.

That's when an explosion of gunfire erupted behind him. One shot zinged past him, whistling so close to his ear he froze, but only for a split second. What pulled him from his momentary paralysis was the second, third and fourth shots.

One of them punched into the back of his triceps, dipping his shoulder and pitching him forward.

He spun and immediately saw his attacker as some strung out kid with bony arms and clothes that looked draped over an emaciated body.

This was the guy who got away. The one in the field Indigo lost two arrows trying to hit. And according to her, he was one of the members of the so called Ophidian Horde who held him captive and threatened his family. Recognition took but a millisecond.

Behind him, Indigo was screaming at the three targets to not move a single muscle or she'd shoot the girl first.

Rex lost track of what was happening very quickly because he was firing off a quick succession of rounds at the clown who got over on him. The sharp echo of a gun of this caliber going off inside a closed, nearly emptied-out store pierced and rattled his brain, something he was used to but never really liked.

The first two rounds hammered the boy's chest, staggering him but not putting him down; the third shot—the kill shot—found its mark. The boy's head snapped backwards and he toppled like a fallen tree.

The bite in Rex's arm had a hot sting to it, and the Ka-bar had fallen from his grip somewhere between him getting shot and him neutralizing his target.

He flexed his fingers on the arm he'd been shot in, cringed at the stab of pain, lamented the stiffness of muscles in revolt. This was the second time he'd been shot today.

In his shot arm, the dull ache he'd managed to stop obsessing over was now throbbing again. Of course, so was his head where he'd been struck. He couldn't give in to the pain this time. He couldn't pass out or complain.

*Pain is not a now thing,* his CO once told him. *Pain is a later thing.*

He needed to cover Indigo. That was the important thing, the right-now thing. Moving as fast as he could to her position, eyes roving everywhere, he found her. She didn't exactly have the situation under control, but she wasn't looking overwhelmed either.

"You don't understand," she was telling one of the two guys who had a gun trained on her. She was looking at him, but one of her guns was on him while the other was aimed low on the girl's torso. "You shoot me, I shoot her in the stomach then you can watch her bleed out slowly as she dies a horrible death."

Rex stepped in...

"Or I kill you and you die anyway," he added, pointing his weapon at the immediate threat. "Either way, this ends up with me using your skull as target practice. Unless you want to be reasonable, which would involve you putting your guns down so we can talk to you the way we intend to talk to you."

"And how's that?" the thug asked, his gun still aimed at Indigo, his eyes as hard as stone and every bit as serious.

"With you pissing your pants and wishing for a weapon, and me and the hottie over there pointing our guns at your man veggies, tiny and insignificant as they may be."

For a second, someone wanted to laugh, he just knew it, but it appeared Rex was the only one appreciating his sense of humor. Then again, he was also the only one of the five of them bleeding. Was there a correlation he was missing? Perhaps. Would he pass out again from the pain of being shot? It was possible. After all, he was a great soldier, but not so great a victim.

"I'm going to count to three, and then I'm going to shoot your little girlfriend here in the ear," Rex said, turning his gun on the girl.

Indigo moved her gun off the girl and now had both guns on the gunman. She looked him straight in the eye and said, "I'm faster than you are, *puta*. With double the load."

"She is," Rex echoed.

The guy finally lowered his gun.

"You know the drill," Indigo said. "Kick them over."

Reluctantly he dropped the weapon, kicked it her way. She

didn't take her eyes off his eyes as she shoved the weapon aside, unconcerned.

"Down on your knees, lace your fingers together and place them behind your head."

With a lot of grumbling and some very colorful language, all three did as they were told.

"The Ophidian Horde," Indigo said. No one looked up. All three of them either looked down or away, confirming what Rex gathered were her suspicions.

Stuffing her weapons into her jeans at the small of her back, she stepped forward, pulled the man's shirt up and saw the tattoo of the black snake in the double S pattern.

"I thought so," she said.

Rex didn't like her being so close to the man and he was prepared to shoot him dead if he so much as flinched in her direction. Fortunately for all of them, he did no such thing.

"Where are the rest of you?" she asked, standing to her full height once more. "Because if this is the whole gang, I'd say you're all pretty pathetic."

The prisoners didn't move, speak, or even look up. Rex was feeling a bit woozy, but fighting it. Before he knew what happened, Indigo had pulled the gun from her pants, spun it around, then pistol-whipped the prisoner on the crown of his head. The man's entire body bucked and a nasty gash opened just beneath his hairline. A stream of blood followed within seconds. He looked up at her, eyes raging, disgusting curses just draining from his mouth.

Rex wasn't surprised by the blood flow; if Indigo was, she didn't show it.

"Are you trying to turn me on?" Rex asked her after the guy finished with his verbal tirade. Now he was really feeling that syrupy fog coming on.

Indigo ignored him.

"Honestly, if that was your intention," Rex replied, "it might be working."

At this point his triceps was really smarting, furthering his agitation. For a second, he couldn't seem to balance out his emotions. He was, in fact, kind of crushing hard on Indigo, but he was also shot and losing blood, and then there was the matter of this taking a long time. Too long. The way the outside world was pushing so mightily at the edges of his vision, how he was starting to feel weak and overcome, he had to speed things up a little or he wouldn't be conscious enough to back Indigo. By passing out, he could be signing her death warrant. His, too.

"I said, where are the rest of you?" Indigo asked.

He said nothing, so Rex shot him in the head, causing everyone to jump. The man slumped over and Indigo turned and fired him a look.

*Did that just happen?*

Woozy, things blurring fast, Rex wobbled backwards a step, caught himself.

"Ask him," Rex said. The blood was now draining from his face. He watched Indigo's eyes drop to the red bloom expanding across his shirt sleeve from where the bullet exited.

"Really?" she said, irritated.

"This is number two, today," he said, sounding not quite himself.

Indigo registered all this with a hint of concern, then she turned to the second man and said, "Answer the question. Now!"

"Just shoot me you stupid bi—"

Her gun was already in his face; her finger was already squeezing the trigger; his head was already rocking back.

She turned and pointed the gun at the girl, who was too freaked out to cry, even though her eyes where filling with tears fast.

"New question," Indigo said.

The bottle blonde with the sloppy body, the heavy makeup and the terrified eyes couldn't stop staring at the two dead men beside her.

"They went easy," Indigo warned the girl, softly, almost

compassionately. "It won't be the same for you. I'll start with your feet and work my way up your body because you're the last. And do you know what they say about the last?"

The girl finally met Indigo's eyes. She looked scared.

"The last ones get it the worst. Which means by the time I'm done with you, you'll be begging for a bullet right in the kisser."

"I'll tell you whatever you want to know," she finally said, tears flooding her eyes.

"Good. First question. Do you have any medical supplies?" By now Rex felt himself leaning on an end-cap, his arm really heavy, his legs feeling a bit gummy.

Indigo looked at him, then back to their impromptu hostage. "Yes."

"On your feet," Indigo barked. "Now!"

The girl was slow to stand. Obviously she was athletically disinclined, as evidenced by balance issues and a lack of coordination when getting up.

She took Indigo and Rex to the employee lounge where there were stacks of all kinds of things, very little of which were edible. Indigo found what she needed.

"Water?" she asked.

"Bottled," the blonde said.

"Get me one."

Rex moved a few things off one of the breakroom tables, then crawled up on it and rolled over on his back.

"Are we bad people, Indigo?" he heard himself ask. "Because they could have been innocent people and we just shot them."

"They weren't innocents," Indigo said, even though she sounded miles away. "Not even close. It's why I've been tracking them."

"I hope you're...right."

When the girl brought the water over, Indigo said, "Open it."

She did.

"Now go stand in that corner, forehead to the wall, and if I see you turn around before I tell you, I'll put two rounds in your spine and leave you to your woes."

The girl started to say something, but thought better of it. Instead, she went to the corner, pressed her face to the wall and stood there.

"And pull up your pants for God's sake. I don't need to be staring at your butt crack the whole time."

Reaching one hand around, the girl hiked up the back of her jeans.

"When I'm done with him," Rex thought he heard Indigo say as the lights in his head were quickly going out, "you're going to tell me everything you know."

At that point, what Rex said next, it could've happened, or perhaps it was all in his head. He wasn't quite sure. Not that it mattered when you're about to pass out. The world around him was closing into a pinhole from the encroaching darkness and he couldn't tell if it was his brain or his mouth doing the talking, but he said it. Or maybe he didn't. The delirium was masking what was real, confusing him, dragging him under.

"I might be falling in love with you."

Those were the words rolling around in his head, or dropping from his mouth. They were cheesy and irrational, but they weren't terribly wrong either.

All he knew was that was the last dominant thought on his mind before his eyes fell shut and the darkness finally closed over him.

# CHAPTER FOUR

Rider strolled confidently through the streets with an AR slung over one shoulder, a Glock on both hips, a spare magazine for each gun on his person, three different knives and two sticks of chewing gum—watermelon flavored.

The second the EMP hit, he put two and two together. It seemed the US government had been overwhelmed by the drones, that they somehow broke free of command. Killing everything with a computer chip was their only option. How far did this reach? For the military to go high altitude with this meant half the country had been effected by the burst. Reason would have it that if half the country was under attack, then why not the whole country?

With precious little information, and a surprising lack of curiosity on his part now that the EMP had fried the grid, he found he didn't really care about the details, important as they may be. The point was, the machines had been stopped. The point was things were about to get really, really bad inside the city.

At least the nuke wasn't detonated at ground level or directly over the city, so barring any unusual weather patterns, he didn't think radiation would be an immediate problem. In the days ahead, he'd have to get a Geiger counter, or a portable multi-channel analyzer, just to be sure.

For the first time in a long time, the former contractor felt his face break into a smile. This was the calm before the storm. He liked calm. He also liked the chaos of the storm. But what sated him most was the level playing field.

Days ago, Rider had been to Dirt Alley where he found Indigo. She was a tough kid, not at all what he expected and certainly able to handle herself in times like these. For now. That much he'd report back. He was heading to home base now, but home base wasn't a house as much as it was a compound: the City College of San Francisco/John Adams Library on Mission and Grove.

He and a couple of guys from the VA found the perfect place to dig in and ride out the collapse of society. Having spent a few years in near isolation, he was comfortable keeping his own company. He knew he should grab a go bag and bug out, but he was a former asset for the dark side of the CIA and war was in his blood. So he stayed. And he gathered a few allies, guys like him, guys who wouldn't run. Guys who liked war.

The college/library was a U shaped structure standing four stories tall. It was solid brick construction, contained multiple defensible points from up high and had chain link fences at the rear. It was already halfway fortified. With enough people from the neighborhood, people who needed shelter and weren't afraid to work hard for others, or fight, they had a safe place to stay, at least until the power was restored.

It could be years. Decades. Or this could just be an isolated event and the National Guard would roll in to assist in the rebuilding of San Francisco.

He tended to think that an EMP blast made things a little more permanent than the average person thought. He wasn't terribly excited about that, but he did like new adventures and new places, and he did thrive when faced with impossible problems, so sadly, there was a part of him that accepted this dark new challenge.

Walking down Masonic Street, two blocks from Grove, he encountered trouble. This wasn't the first time, and it wouldn't be the last. The problem with lawlessness was that the dregs of society always had a way of being everywhere, in everyone's business. And no matter how hard you tried to avoid them, some circumstances just didn't allow for it.

The instant these guys saw him (he counted six total), they nodded his way and changed their gait, which became predictably thuggish. Great, he thought. Awesome. One of them pulled out a pistol, walked with it at his side. This must be the leader.

Rider never once broke stride, nor did he draw a weapon. If he played his cards right, he could get past them without incident. It wasn't looking likely though.

Rider slid his hand into his pocket and brought out a fresh stick of gum. He unwrapped the stick, spit the over-chewed nub in his mouth into the foil, then rolled it up and shoved it in his pocket. When he slid the fresh stick in his mouth, it was an amazing burst of fruity flavor, the third best thing that happened to him that day.

Chewing his gum, getting it soft in his mouth, his eyes worked quickly to assess his surroundings. The six of them were fifty feet away and closing. Each of them wore dark sunglasses and each of them looked like they were strapped, even though the lead was the only one with his gun pulled.

Yeah, this was going to be a problem.

He'd just passed the baseball field, which had fifty or sixty foot nets and limited entry points, if any; he was now heading into a full residential block of only decorative trees and a few cars for cover, so this wasn't looking so promising either.

Eyes roving, all he saw were alcoves to front doors that weren't deep, and garage doors that were flush with the house. To make matters worse, each house was like so many other houses here in that they were on zero lot lines with shared walls, which meant no escape alleys or places for cover if a shootout unfolded.

A Chinese woman with her small son opened her front door, saw him and startled. "Get back inside, lock your doors," he said.

She did as instructed.

The six guys fanned out so he couldn't pass them on the sidewalk. He thought about stepping off into the street where a Honda Accord had slammed into a lifted Chevy Silverado and was abandoned.

It wouldn't work for cover for long, though, so he decided to meet the pack head on.

"Afternoon fellas," he said.

"Whatchu doin' pops?" the lead clown asked. Black or tan slacks, white button ups, slicked back hair and tattoos—these guys were low-level foot soldiers out on patrol.

"Just passing through," he said, ignoring the comment about his age. "You?"

"Expanding our influence," the lead said, pushing the words on him like a stiff shove. Then, with a fake smile, he said, "And for that we need weapons and ammo."

"I have both," Rider offered knowing exactly where this was going.

"No kidding, *ese,*" one mumbled, causing the others to snicker.

Subtly, the group pulled in closer to make a smiley-face mouth around him. It wasn't a huge, sweeping smile, but it was enough to tell him they weren't your garden variety meat heads.

Tilting his head, reaching over his shoulder, he lifted the modified AR-15 off his back, set it on the ground between them to the left. He unholstered his two Glocks, laid them down on the sidewalk as well, one on either side of his feet. After that he put two of the three knives on the ground and then, from his pocket, his last foil-wrapped piece of chewing gum.

When he glanced up, they were all looking at each other like they couldn't believe how easy it was. But none of this was going to be easy for them. Himself included.

"That's it?" one said.

"That's it," he replied with an easy smile.

"You've still got one more knife," the lead said, using his weapon as a pointer. He was pointing at the eight inch blade on Rider's hip. "Set it down there with the others."

"I have a bullet lodged in my right leg," Rider lied. "I need the knife to dig it out when I get to where I'm going."

"Which is where?"

"None of your business," he said, politely.

"Well I'm sure they have knives where you're headed, so just put that one down and you can move on."

"I'd love to, since you seem like nice kids," he said, getting frowns and a few disbelieving chortles, "but this knife is staying with me."

"Kick the weapons to us," one of them barked, pointing at his guns. The lead was probably five feet away. He was at least eight feet from the guys flanking him.

"What's your name?" Rider asked, looking only at him, not the others.

"Roberto," he said.

"You're not a very good listener, Bob," Rider said. "Does your old lady tell you that? If she does, then she's a keeper because man, *it's true.*"

Now comes the posturing, the mean-mugging, the threatening weapon routine. Roberto pointed his gun right at Rider and said, "Now *puta.*"

Taking a deep breath, aware of every single muscle in his body and mentally supercharging them, he calmly said, "My sight's not so good, cataracts in my left eye, shrapnel in my right, but are you pointing a gun at me? Because I gave you my guns already."

"Kick them here!" he barked.

"Let me say this for the cheap seats," Rider said, his impatience showing. "I have a bullet lodged in my right leg, so if I try to kick anything, I'm pretty sure the pain will make me pass out. And if I try to kick with my left, I'll have to stand on my right, which will surely buckle. So let me reiterate this as politely as I can, take my weapons if you want, take my life if you need to, but I can't have this bullet in my leg much longer without risking infection so stop asking for my knife and just take what I gave you."

Roberto pulled back the slide, chambered a round.

"I ain't asking no more, pops," he warned. "Kick the weapons our way, with or without your gimp leg."

"No."

For what felt like five lifetimes they stood there. Rider didn't back down; they didn't back down. No one even blinked. Finally one of the guys from the peanut gallery chimed in.

"He's just an old man."

"Don't let the gray hair fool you, *ese,*" Roberto said. "He's young. Forty maybe, forty-five."

"Fifty-three," Rider lied. In truth, he was ten years younger than he'd just claimed and in excellent shape.

One of the guys said, "I can't tell if he's ex-military or a male model."

The five of them had a laugh, but Roberto failed to see the humor. He was the one Rider worried about most.

"Male model," Rider lied. "But don't go getting your hopes up fellas. I'm a girls-only kind of guy." Fake-hobbling back a step, Rider motioned to the weapons and said, "Have at them. I even left a piece of gum there for the soft looking kid on the end."

"Ain't no one soft here but you, *cabrón,*" Roberto said. "Turn around and walk your dumb ass away."

"I'm not going that way, Bob," Rider responded. Giving a forward nod, he said, "I'm headed that way, and right now you're blocking me. Also, keep in mind I was minding my own business when you came up on me. If you want my weapons, I've given them to you. But if you want to sit around in some sort of testos-

terone-laden circle jerk, honestly, you can do that all by your-
selves without me having to watch, so do your thing already then
get the hell out of the way."

Annoyed, but bested, Roberto stowed his gun in his slacks at
the small of his back then stepped forward and grabbed the AR.
The minute Roberto bent down, Rider grabbed his knife and in
an almost otherworldly display of speed and precision, he blew
past Roberto, but not before trenching open the man's carotid
artery with a ferocious sweep of the blade.

Rider was suddenly in the mix of the other five thugs who
were scrambling for position. Time compressed itself and all he
saw were targets, moves and the end result: all of them all being
dead in a very specific order.

Gunfire shattered the silence, but not before Rider ducked a
punch from the outside man, swung around and grabbed a hold
of his Adam's apple. He used the guy as his shield. To the left of
him Roberto was cupping a hand over his wounded neck, but
blood was pulsing out from between his fingers. He staggered
backwards and forwards, like a drunk. He tried to speak but
nothing came out.

"Cat got your tongue, Bob?" Rider said.

In one final attempt to go out like a true gangster, Roberto
shot through his own man trying to hit Rider. Two of the three
shots punched through Rider's human shield and struck him in
the chest. The lightweight body armor he was wearing absorbed
the lead, but not before exacting a small toll.

*What in God's name is he shooting?* Rider wondered, catching his
breath.

His human shield was hobbling on wonky knees and there
were still four guys left. All of them were weapons hot and he
had a knife, an almost dead guy for protection, and a fresh stick
of gum. Not all was lost, but he hadn't seen it play out like this.
Then again, in a fight, sometimes you have to operate on the fly.

The second he felt the last of his human shield's strength go,
Rider dove in Roberto's direction, rolling and then launching up

on him hard. Gunfire peppered the air. He felt several nips and bites, but this wasn't the first time he'd been shot under fire. In seconds flat, his knife was up under Roberto's chin. The man stiffed. Internalizing his own injuries, Rider decided none of the rounds that hit him stuck too hard, but damn, some of that lead hurt pretty good.

He was still on his feet though, and now he had a new human shield: Roberto. Bob. Blood was pumping from the man's neck, a veritable fountain of red, albeit not as vigorous as before. It wouldn't be long before this human shield went the way of the last.

"Is this a Mexican stand-off we're in?" Rider quipped, looking at the other guys. "Or do you care as much for him as he did for your compadre, the guy he just shot trying to shoot me?"

Blood soaked slurs poured from the mouth of the twenty-something Hispanic dying in his arms. Seconds had passed at this point; Roberto had precious few left.

Already his body was getting heavy.

Grabbing the weapon tucked in Roberto's waistband, Rider open fired and hit three of the remaining four thugs. The chamber clicked twice on the fourth man.

*Damn.*

The fourth man open fired, hitting Roberto, and by proxy, hitting Rider. Each round kicked a little harder than the last, but the vest held even if it felt like his bones weren't holding up the same.

Finally the fourth man's chamber ran dry and Rider could no longer manage the dead man. He stepped backwards and shoved Roberto's corpse aside.

The last clown standing was frantically reloading his weapon, but Rider grabbed one of his Glocks off the sidewalk and leveled it on the man. "You have three moves here, son."

"Yeah?" the kid replied, still loading his weapon.

"First, keep loading that gun and I'm going to shoot you in the face and be done with it."

He stopped.

"What's your name?" Rider asked.

"Why?"

"I'm curious by nature," he said.

"Alejandro."

"Like the Lady Gaga song? That Alejandro?" The street soldier rolled his eyes, which caused Rider to smirk. "Well, Ali-Ali-jandro, there are two more options."

Still holding the gun, but poised for battle, he said, "Option two?"

"You walk away and wipe your hands of these flunkies. You lose your friends and this fight, but you keep your life."

"And if my pride makes this an impossible choice?" he asked, eyes diamond hard and roasting with hatred.

"Well then I'll let you choose one of my two knives and we can go hand-to-hand like civilized gents," Rider said looking extra dignified.

"You killed them all," Alejandro said, still reeling.

Now Rider's mouth became a flat, emotionless slash. "All of you were dead the minute you stopped me, you just didn't know it yet."

"So you think I should walk away?"

"I do."

"And you won't shoot me in the back?"

"Depends," he said.

"On?"

"On how much longer you want to stand here gossiping like a pair of school girls. Make a decision, Ali-Ali-jandro. Now."

"You really got a bullet in your right leg?" he asked, looking down.

"No."

Tucking his gun in the front of his trousers, he burned Rider with his eyes and said, "This isn't over, pops. We're building an army, and when—"

The bullet plowing through the kid's brain stopped his

mouth from working. Wide eyed with death, he fell to the side-walk in a heap.

"Your threats are duly noted," Rider mumbled, sitting down beside the slumped over Roberto and in half the coward's blood supply.

Roberto's expanding red pond was generous, but it failed to reach Rider's guns, and by proxy, his last stick of gum. Thank God. Despite the wrapper being flecked with blood spatter, he peeled back the foil and stuck his last piece in his mouth, chewing loudly before adding one softened wad to the other.

Blowing bubbles, he swept up his guns, then got to his feet.

There was something about the fake watermelon flavor that was downright amazing for the first twenty or so minutes. He was inside that window of happiness with enough time left to get back home.

Stripping the dead of their weapons, and one man of his long sleeved button up (it was the least blood stained), Rider stacked the bodies in front of a blue and white garage door like the garbage they were. He then began loading the hardware into the stolen shirt.

Things started to hurt. He was missing bits of flesh here and there. He wasn't sure what hurt more, being grazed a few times, or taking three rounds in the vest. Either way, by tomorrow morning he was going to be red welts and a patchwork of black and blue bruises that would turn green and yellow in the days to come.

Tying up the shirt's arms to contain the cradle of weapons, Rider hoisted them over his shoulder and walked the remaining two blocks where his buddy in an old red and white Chevy stood patrol at the street corner.

"Rider," he said.

"Waylon."

"You alright?" he asked.

"Gonna need a Band-Aid and some whiskey," Rider replied,

limping a bit on his left leg where one of the bullets blazed a burn trail over his thigh.

"That racket up the street," he said, "was that you?"

"Yeah."

"Problem solved?"

"For now," Rider replied, still walking.

"There gonna be blowback?"

"Maybe," he said, limp-walking up the road, his back to his friend. "Probably."

"You shot?" he called up.

"Couple times, yeah."

"Go see Sarah," Waylon said, to which Rider replied, "Heading there now."

Not looking back, Rider made his way up to the back fence where he was let inside the compound by a woman with a gun and no sense of humor on account of her entire family perishing in a car fire.

He made his way to the makeshift triage center/infirmary to have his wounds looked at. Sure enough, his chest was a smattering of bruises and he was hit in the same leg twice. Nothing serious though, just a couple of red trenches.

Still, it was troubling that he'd been shot at all. Maybe he really was getting old.

Old and slow.

Then again, the way Sarah Richards was looking at him (she was the dewy looking beauty working on him—a twenty-four year old nursing student from Cuba, and the closest thing they had to a doctor), he realized that even slowing down a bit, not all was lost.

With his injuries cared for and Sarah looking a little flush as he put his shirt back on, he said, "Many thanks, Doc," which she liked.

"Are you doing anything later?" she asked, cleaning up the small stack of bloody gauze.

It wasn't an invitation, Rider knew—she was simply making

conversation. Giving her a long second look, he realized just how attractive she was, and not for the first time.

Like his second ex-wife said, he wasn't one for romance. He was just better at killing things. Maybe with Sarah, if he ever had the opportunity, he'd give romance one more try. Or maybe he'd just go out and shoot some more bad guys and not think about this kind of thing ever again.

"Gonna check in on our mystery guest right now," he finally said. "She awake yet?"

"Not yet," Sarah replied. "Maybe tonight."

"Vitals though?" he asked.

"Steady."

"Do I have to keep getting shot to see you, or would you be up for an evening stroll a bit later?"

Now she turned and looked at him.

"You don't think you're too old for me?" she asked.

"Of course I do," he replied.

"You've been shot."

"Haven't forgotten about that," he said.

"Yet you're asking me out on a walk anyway?" she said, looking extra shy and ridiculously cute doing so.

"I am."

Her head started to nod on its own as she tried on the idea, and then she said, "Yeah, I'd like that. We haven't really gotten to know each other."

"Not on a social level, no," he said. "I'll swing by your room around eight?"

"If your leg doesn't freeze up on you, then yes, eight is good."

"Now about our mystery patient..."

# CHAPTER FIVE

Rider headed into the next room where the woman lay in a bed, her head bandaged, yellow and green circles under her eyes. Her nose was broken, but reset. Her head wounds treated.

When he found her she was in a seven car pile up with the cars in front of her and behind her in flames. Drone attack. When all this happened, Rider was downtown. He was just walking, which was something he often did to clear his mind.

If not for the routine, the almost aimlessness of it, he would probably begin to go crazy. He was a former operator, a contract killer for the CIA, and now retired. He left the company gracefully, but the truth was, he both hated and loved the chaos he left behind. The strange dichotomy was the basis of many a conversation with many a post-service shrink.

In the end, he stopped going to therapy because he realized he was a natural magnet for pandemonium. If not in the battlefield, then in the business world; and if not in the business world, then in the bedroom. In the end, he gave up the women and the work in favor of making ends meet on simpler terms. To do this he bought and sold various items on Craigslist as a means of affording his Spartan lifestyle. There was never any comfort in it. He loved almost nothing about his life. It was almost as if he were waiting for something to come along and take him from all this monotony. That something happened to be a drone strike on the city.

Armageddon.

When he'd come upon the pile-up of vehicles, he moved from car to car checking the bodies. When he got to the woman, he'd stopped. She was a looker. But dead. He almost moved on, but he didn't. It wasn't because of her good looks, it was because he caught a glimpse of a very weak pulse beating in her neck.

*As good as dead,* he thought.

Or not.

Standing there in that moment, thinking about all the lives he'd taken over the years, he realized it was high time he try to balance the scales and save a few, even if the effort seemed futile. Certain the drones had gone, he looked in on the woman with greater focus.

The airbag had gone off and hit her in the face, breaking her nose. Another car had t-boned her on the driver's side. The driver of the offending car (a twenty-something Asian kid with half his face ripped off) had flown through the windshield and slammed head-first into the side of this woman's A pillar. Looking at the kid's car, he saw no airbags. An unbuckled seat-belt. His neck was broken in half and lolling to the side at an extremely unnatural angle. The eye that was least damaged was open wide, glassed over with death.

When he dragged the boy's ravaged body out of the way, the woman in the car moved just enough to let him know she wasn't a lost cause after all.

The driver's side window was glass shards everywhere. Blonde hair was matted red. The woman's nose was slightly crooked, twin streams of blood flooding her generous lips, staining her perfectly white teeth in splotchy dollops of crimson.

For a second he saw her nice clothes, her jewelry, her mani-cured nails and he almost left her. He hated that sometimes he thought like that, but he did. His experiences with wealthy women were varied, none of them good.

Would this be different?

At this point, the fires in front of and behind her car were spreading. The bodies inside these automobiles were engulfed in flames, and it reminded him of the war overseas, of a village he and his team once cleared using M4A1's and napalm.

Looking away, forcing himself to grab the woman and carry her to safety, he wondered if saving her might relieve a bit of the karmic burden now plaguing him daily.

Standing in that village, he'd watched the bodies burn, and he did nothing.

Back then, he'd been remiss to save a single soul. Not because he didn't want to, but because the death of innocents was the cruel message they were sending. It turned out, the message meant for someone else was seared so permanently into his mind that not a day went by when he wasn't tortured by these memories.

Self-loathing often made him careless with his life which, in turn, took his hard edges and made them razor sharp. He was an efficient killer only because he had so much pain and rage inside him that when it came out, often the only thing left behind were tarns of blood, and a stack of bodies. He was a smile on the outside, a calm demeanor, a man at peace with his surroundings. But inside, he was barely held together and only by the sheer force of will alone.

Then along came this woman...

She weighed nothing in his arms as he carried her to the compound. He knew they had a doctor there, a student rather, and he knew this was his only chance to get the woman the medical attention she needed.

Her injuries were superficial by the look of it, but beyond that he didn't know what kind of internal bleeding she might have and he wasn't about to inspect her without her permission, which she couldn't give to him while unconscious.

Two or three times she woke up, coughing, crying, mumbling incoherently. He simply did the best he could to reassure her, and to get her to safety as quickly as possible. It was no easy task and twice they were nearly eviscerated by drones.

He got her to the college though, to the doctor. The doctor, of course, had been Sarah. Sarah whose name he hadn't known just yet. On the bed, the young doctor said, "Wow, she's beautiful," to which Rider said, "True beauty lies beneath the skin. She could be the ugliest woman you'll ever meet and we wouldn't know it until she speaks."

"Do you think we should let her die?" Sarah asked, deadpan, but stopping what she was doing to look up at Rider.

"I have a quarter," he said, matching her expression. "We can flip, if you want."

"Okay," she said. "You flip it, I'll call it."

He took the coin, flipped it in the air and she called heads. It was heads. "So normally I wouldn't have you do this, but there's no one else I really know, and you're the one who brought her here…"

"What are you asking?"

"I need to inspect her body, and I need your help. We have to check for cuts, lacerations, indications of internal bleeding—"

"I thought you could do that, you're the doctor. I'm just…I'm just a good Samaritan who didn't ask for any of this."

Ignoring him, she lifted the woman's sweater. Her stomach was flat, flawless, her breasts small but cupped nicely by an expensive, bejeweled bra. Rider looked away, uncomfortable. He felt Sarah look up at him, thought she might've smiled.

"You gay?"

"If I was," he replied, "I wouldn't look away."

"She's unconscious," Sarah said, examining her body. "She's not going to mind." When she pulled the shirt back down, she said, "We have to turn her over."

They did.

Again, she lifted the woman's shirt and checked her torso.

There were bruises, but they were external. Nothing appeared to be broken.

"My name is Rider," he'd said to Sarah, awkward.

"Got a last name?"

"Not really."

"Well it's a good name," she replied. Back then, she didn't give her name and he didn't ask. He preferred to just call her "Doc" and she seemed to like it just fine.

"I'm not a real doctor you know," she said. "I'm just a second year."

"Well I'm not a real rider. I'm just a guy. If my name was any indication of what I do, it would be Walker, but that sounds too much like *The Walking Dead* and I don't want anyone thinking of me as a zombie, even though most days that's exactly how I feel."

If he was named for what he did, in all honesty he'd be called Killer, but no one really ever gets that special feeling for you if your name is synonymous with murder.

He smiled; she smiled.

That was that.

Over the days, he came to see this mystery woman, but she was sleeping a lot. She'd had a concussion, a broken nose (which he helped the doctor reset that day), lacerations on the side of her head and burns on her face and forearms from the airbag deploying.

Yet she was still an attractive woman.

He never stared at her for too long because in times of war, you don't obsess over women as much as you do your best to survive. Women were a distraction, and he was in war mode.

Sometimes, though, he looked at her thoughtfully. Tried to imagine what she was like inside. Tried to guess at who she'd been in the real world.

Shaking his head more times than not, he thought, *this woman is taking me places I can't afford to go just yet.* And the doctor? She was no help either. She was easy on the eyes as well, competent and witty, blessed with a lighthearted sense of humor that came off as something of a miracle considering the absolute hell they were under.

But she was young. Too young.

That's why Rider eventually left the compound. Well, that and one other reason. The mystery woman, in one of her waking moments, was asking for someone. She was repeating a name. Rider put his ear close to her mouth, caught the name, then asked where she was and the woman told him. Because he was growing fond of Sarah, because he found himself thinking more about her and their patient than surviving, he needed to go, to walk, to have a mission.

Finding this girl was his mission.

Indigo.

After a few days he found her, but he didn't want to bring her back to the compound because she was a girl who was surviving on her own just fine. The girl was every bit as competent as Sarah, just younger. Less jovial. If he took her from her home, everything she was developing in herself would come to a swift and jarring halt. The last thing this world needed, Rider had been thinking to himself, was another follower.

He recognized in this teenager true survivability and this made him want to check back in on her. He had people at the compound to take care of though, friends to help, responsibilities that had his name written on them.

They say inside of a year, after the grid goes down, power goes out and society is thrust headlong into the dark ages, most of the population dies. This is no real news. Certainly not to a guy like Rider.

What they don't tell you is how all these people come to die. What happens to them when they get hungry, when they need a place to stay, when supplies run out and food goes rotten and clean water and functional sewage systems are a thing of the past. What they don't say is that people will always fall back to their base instincts and that's when you separate the wheat from the chaff, the wolves from the sheep. Rider was a wolf. He would survive.

But everyone else?

Well, he thought, it was best not to get too attached.

Yet there he was, getting attached. He'd just asked Sarah out for a walk and now he was here with the woman whose name he still didn't know. There was a ring on her finger, but when he found Indigo, there was no father figure around. It was just her.

The woman slowly worked her eyes open. One of them was shot through with red from the trauma to her head, but not like before. She was looking a lot better. Nearly perfect.

"You," she said.

"Me."

"I dreamt of you," she said, groggy.

"I'm afraid your dreams might be mixing with reality, which has become somewhat of a nightmare of late."

"So I know you?"

"Not really."

"But you know me?" she asked.

"Not really."

"Why are you here then?" she said, her eyes heavy, her body willing her back to sleep.

"I'm the one who brought you here," he said, grinding his molars because honestly he didn't want to admit that. To admit he had saved her would be binding them together, and having people bound to you was crippling. At least, that's how it felt to Rider.

"You saved me?" she asked, her voice scratchy, her eyes full of foggy wonder.

"It was nothing," he said. "The effort, I mean. All life has value and yours needed saving."

She took his hand, and it was soft—the skin of her hand on his. He hadn't held a woman's hand in well over a year, so experiencing the rapture of human touch was both heart rending and uncomfortable. He inched his hand out of hers then she settled back down, the effort having sapped most of her energy.

"Am I okay?" she asked.

"Yes."

"I don't feel well, though," she all but whispered.

"You had a concussion, a broken nose, some bruising. Do cuts heal slowly for you? Or burns? Things like that?"

"Before, no. I used to heal just fine. But now, yes, things have slowed down significantly."

Her face was profound sadness. He didn't understand.

"What do you mean?" he forced himself to ask.

Looking right into his eyes and not blinking, she said, "Please don't take this the wrong way, because I'm grateful for you and what you've done, but I have cancer. I was already dying before you found me."

Now he sagged into his body so hard it made him not only mad about this life, but enthusiastically pissed off that he opened that part of himself up to care about a woman who was going to die anyway.

"You're still young," he said, his voice tender, unguarded.

She swallowed hard, cleared her throat, then looked at him and said, "Cancer doesn't care if you're forty or eighty, or even ten for that matter."

"People are beating it though," he said, sounding desperate even to himself. "There's a chance, right?"

"Where am I?" she finally asked, looking around. "This doesn't look like a hospital."

"Do you even know what's going on out there?"

"I'm not sure," she admitted.

"The drones, the city, the AI? Any of that ring a bell?" he asked, looking right at her, not knowing how to delicately put the fact that society as they knew it had been crushed under the boot of innovation and technological advancement.

"What's AI?"

"Artificial Intelligence."

"How does any of this explain why I'm here?" she said, her eyes so heavy, her petite body growing so still he wondered if she even bore the strength necessary to hear and comprehend what he had to say. In the end, he decided the truth would be too traumatizing. He'd wait a few days, fill her in on things then.

"When you're feeling rested, I'll tell you, but for now, just sleep."

She reached out, rested her hand on his forearm and closed her eyes. "Thank you for what you did."

And then she drifted off to sleep again, her breathing deepening, her body once again finding reprieve in its slumber. He sat with her for the better part of an hour until Sarah came in and said, "Did you get a chance to talk to her?"

"I did," he said.

"And?"

"I wish I would have never saved her."

# CHAPTER SIX

Raymond King, a.k.a. "Kingpin Ray," sat at a large desk in the enormous Sutter Health building on California and Cherry with his fingers tented and his three generals standing before him. A bottle of Scotch stood open and breathing, but as much as he enjoyed the idea of the finer things in life, what he really wanted was the power back and an ice cold Corona.

Times were changing, though. He had to change with them.

If he played his cards right, he would command an army by the month's end, and at the head of this army stood his enforcers, all reliable men, all loyal beyond measure.

Looking around he said, "Am I to assume you want to rule this city by force?"

Salazar said, "Indeed."

Salazar was his most loyal man, his chief enforcer and a friend. He was not seeing the bigger picture though, and King intended to be clear. "In a city that's been overwhelmed by force, what you need to lead *is not more force*."

"We're a gang," Salazar argued. "We control things, we sell things, we kill things if necessary. These are the basic tenants we agreed to when forming The Ophidian Horde."

King finally took a sip of the Scotch, let it warm his throat and belly, then said, "One of the first things I learned when reading Sun Tzu's *Art of War* was to read the landscape. Do you think the landscape now is the same as it was a month ago?"

"Obviously not."

"Outwardly, we appeal to the people. From there we will create our own landscape from which to dominate."

"We're not politicians," Salazar snipped, causing the other two enforcers to give a unifying nod.

"True, we're less corrupt, I'll give you that. But that isn't the point."

"You want to use the carrot not the stick," Salazar said.

"No, I want to be more like the pied piper. We'll sell safety. We'll sell security. And when the time is right, we'll have everything we want, but with the cooperation of the people, not the pushback."

"Why must we rely upon benevolence as a measure of control when weapons work so much better?"

"Do you have a problem with that?" he asked.

"Others will."

King shifted in his chair, took another shot. "Those who don't do it our way, those within our ranks anyway, they are to be killed on site. Compliance will surely follow. We are not one gang but the dissidents of many. I don't expect everyone to see it my way just yet, but they will and you will help them."

Salazar now stood uncomfortably on his feet. King knew it would come to this. The sooner they discussed this the better.

"We're not the only outfit here, King."

"That goes without saying."

"What about their captains? Their lieutenants? Their soldiers? With them, you don't just lop off the head and expect the body to die with it. You lop off the head and expect another, more grislier head to grow back."

"All the other gangs will fall if we do this right. We'll sweep in the soldiers, the lieutenants, the captains if need be. Collect all those willing to share the vision."

"What you're suggesting is starting a war of epic proportion," Gomez said. He was the newest of King's enforcers, a fierce man, an unwavering man.

"This is the single most important power grab we'll ever have at our disposal," King said. "If you think they're thinking anything different, if you think they're not in some place exactly like this planning our swift demise, they you are gravely mistaken and in no way deserving of the position I've provided you."

Kingpin Ray watched his right hand man grinding his molars. Finally Salazar drew a short, sharp breath through his nose and lifted his chin. "So we are going to be soft to the people, but hard with our rivals?"

"This is a new world and we have to be a new gang. So yes."

Salazar ripped his .45 loose, fired two quick rounds into Raymond King's head. His friend's skull snapped back, two smoking holes in his forehead, and then he slumped over sideways and that was that.

Salazar was the ranking enforcer, so with King dead, he took King's place. Yelling at his friend's corpse, accentuating his points with the thrust of his smoking gun, he said, "We are going to be hard *all* the time! This city does not need benevolence right now, they need a leader who is not afraid to make tough choices!"

From behind Salazar, a shot was fired and the man's forehead blew open a wash of red. He fell face first on the ground with a sick thump.

Gomez and Gunderson both spun around, weapons drawn. They stopped when they saw who was standing before them. The killer said nothing. There was no posturing, no grandstanding, no words wasted on people not interested in listening.

"Do either of you wish to challenge me?" he asked with a soft voice. Neither Gomez nor Gunderson moved. "No? Good. There are community events rising up across the city. We will visit them, introduce ourselves, and we will do what we've always done, but with the chains off. We took the police stations. They are no more. There is no law, no national guard, no courts or jails. There is only kill or be killed. These people need to know that we will kill how and when we like and there is nothing they can do about it."

"Are you planning on leading this gang?"

"Yes."

"But, you're a hitman."

"And you're politicians with guns."

Gomez and Gunderson exchanged looks. Then Gunderson said, "So we just show up and kill them and that's it?"

"No, you kill the men and the children, but you take the women. The women are ours. The spoils of war."

"Kill the children?" Gomez asked. "Are you *pinche loco?*"

The bullet blew out Gomez's front teeth, wobbling him, but not killing him right away. Gunderson neither jumped nor panicked. He just turned and watched Gomez choke to death, wide-eyed and scared, standing on soft knees and buckling legs. Blood leaked from the lower half of his face as he stumbled to a nearby chair, fell into it then slumped over and died.

"Is this going to be a problem for you?" the hitman asked Gunderson.

Gunderson was not a man not to be trifled with, but he was not consumed by ego, either. He was a soldier at heart, willing and able to take orders, and more than respectful of the chain of command.

"No. No problem here."

"I'm pleased to hear that, Mr. Gunderson."

"Can I ask you a question?" he asked. The former hitman waited. "What do I call you?"

"The only name people need to know is *our* name."

"The Ophidian Horde."

"In this day and age, under these uncertain circumstances, benevolence and diplomacy don't work. We're on a clock. If we don't take the upper hand while our enemies are regrouping, we will be like these *cabróns* here: shot dead and forgotten."

"I'll handle it."

"See that you do," he said as he turned and disappeared down the hall.

Gunderson looked at the dead men before him. Instead of cleaning them up, he simply took the opened bottle of Scotch and all of their guns, then left the office, shutting the door behind him. Thinking of the man who just assumed control of The Ophidian Horde, he couldn't help the involuntary shiver that ran through him. This contract killer was a slight Guatemalan man with no conscience, no hesitation, and absolute surety in his every move, as to be expected. Gunderson realized it was best to make a man like this a friend because so far, three of his friends had been disposed of already, and he wasn't anxious to be next.

# CHAPTER SEVEN

When the drones set in on the city, blowing up cars and buildings and people, Chad and Wagner thought the best thing to do was start building bombs. How else were they supposed to stop the machines?

"We need focus," Chad said.

"No," Wagner replied, "we need to chill."

"What exactly do you have in mind?" Chad asked, anxious, giddy almost.

Chad looked young, too tall for the age of his face, and too much hair for a normal kid. It was long and brown; it was halfway down his neck at the back and falling in his eyes in the front. He lived out of saggy jeans and decorative t-shirts his mother bought him from second hand stores and Walmart when they were on sale for six dollars plus tax.

Wagner, a Japanese/American kid with a similar mop of hair —his perfectly straight with chopped edges he called geometric funk—said, "Let me tell you what I have in mind. For starters, it's three choices."

He pulled out three clear baggies and some rolling papers. On the baggies were white labels with names inked on them.

The big question wasn't which baggie were they going to smoke. It was which order were they going to smoke *all* the baggies.

"Behind door number one," Wagner announced, "we have Grandberry Skunkhound."

"A fine choice," Chad said.

"Behind door number two is my personal favorite, Plunkbottom Diesel."

"You have exceptional taste, my friend," Chad said in a theatrical tone, grinning and staring at baggie number three while rubbing his hands together.

"Indeed I do. And that's why I have door number three. Bubblegum Swamp Kush. This little dreamboat," Wagner said, dangling the clear plastic baggie between them, "is reportedly an eighty percent indica strain from Bulldog Seeds in the Netherlands. Take special care and attention to the frosty, resinous buds."

Chad leaned forward for a sniff, but Wagner pulled the baggie back, ever so slightly. "In case you're wondering, and I know you are, the Bubblegum Swamp Kush has a sour taste and smell to it, and its THC content is a gnat's hair south of twenty percent."

"In other words," Chad said, "we'd best take this party to the couch, turn on some TV and just *chill*…"

"Brainstorming session begins right after we roll up two big fat fatties."

Chad and Wagner smoked to relax, but they nearly relaxed themselves into a coma and there was work to do, so they cut a few lines of coke to even things out. Chad ate a bag of Doritos and played *Call of Duty* while Wagner stayed up all night moving through the dark web in various chat rooms of friends of friends.

"You buying more?" Chad asked. "Because…*wow.*"

"Trying to figure out how to make bombs."

"We got plenty of bongs man. One for every strain. Which reminds me…"

"Bombs, as in *kaboom!*" Wagner said. "Those kinds of bombs."

"Bro, we ain't like that. Look at us. We're mellow. Besides, what in Jesus' name would we blow up anyway?"

"When you have the problem of building bombs resolved," Wagner said, his fingers flying across the keyboard about a thousand miles an hour, "finding targets becomes easy. Is your laptop still operational?"

"Last I checked," he said, half his body on the couch, an arm and a leg draped over. "Hey, where'd my other sock go?" He just realized his foot was cold. The right one not the left. As it happened, both socks were on his left foot.

"Your left foot was cold," Wagner said over his shoulder. "I need you to jump online and see what you can find out about building timers."

"I don't think we can smoke and snort together anymore."

"Timers, Chad. Timers."

"Yeah dude, I got it," he said. "Timers."

Wagner learned how to make bombs with normal household products and some gunpowder, while Chad finally took on the task of learning how to make the timers.

Whenever they struck that perfect balance between too chill and too strung out, they brainstormed about how to turn one bomb into a larger bomb by piggybacking onto things that could be turned into even larger bombs.

"Propane trucks," Chad blurted out.

"Not common," Wagner said with an eye roll. "But your regular everyday car...super common."

"Really?" Chad quipped.

"No, dummy. It's hard to find cars these days. Especially on the streets and in people's garages. Of course it's common. Like looking outside and seeing blue skies."

"It's all smoke these days, bro."

"Focus, man," Wagner said. Snapping his fingers he said, "Eyes on the prize."

"Gas stations," Chad said. "You get like three or four pumps wired up, the explosion would wipe out everything but a person's shadow."

Wagner turned and fired him a look. "Is that a Hiroshima reference?"

"What else?" Chad asked, chortling.

"Nothing, just see how to build timers. See what we need. Make a list of parts and stuff. Then we can figure out where they're sold and go shopping."

"Brotatochip, I can't even walk a straight line. I'm so wide awake and exhausted at the same time, it's like one side of my head is kicking the other side in the balls."

"That doesn't even make sense," Wagner said.

"You look like your dad right now. It's...uncanny."

"You've never even seen my dad."

"Whatever," Chad said. "The point is, I need some sleep, but I'm going to need some of that Plunkbottom Diesel to pump the brakes first."

Clicking the window shut, shutting off the monitor, Wagner spun his chair around and said, "I could use a soft landing myself."

"So?" Chad said.

"Ask and ye shall receive," Wagner replied, grabbing the baggie. The two of them smoked and laughed and sank into the couch, an easy haze washing over them, pulling them under to places where their dreams were bigger and more colorful, like something you would see if you were on acid, or a sociopath.

"I feel like Jeffrey Dahmer," Chad said.

"Dahmer's dead."

"Yes, but I'm very, very alive, but also not at the same time."

---

The next day, when they woke enough to smell their filthy breaths and their four day old clothes, they realized the power was out. Wagner was slow to the jump, but steady in his assessment.

"We're screwed. Must've blown a fuse or something."

But they didn't. Everything was fried: the TV, the computers, their cell phones and their brains.

"The drones must have hit the power station, or something like that. You have the list, right Chad? The stuff we need?"

They looked for awhile before finding a list folded to the size of a quarter and stuck in between the double layer of socks that was now on Chad's sweaty foot.

They spent the day on their bicycles smoking pot and marveling at how nothing seemed to work. There were people in the streets, abandoned cars, drones littering the ground in some places, as if they'd just fallen from the sky. They dragged one behind their bikes for awhile, but it was too heavy, too awkward, so they let it go.

"It's like God snapped his fingers and all the commotion came to a stop," Chad said, marveling at the sheer destruction everywhere, especially to the downed drones.

"This is Biblical man."

"For sure."

Over the next forty hours, they smoked even more as they constructed a small stack of pipe bombs. And then they ate the rest of their snacks and decided if they didn't have munchies, they couldn't smoke. Simple as that. So then they lit up one last joint and romanced the hell out of it.

Wagner looked up at Chad and said, "What should we do?"

Chad shrugged his shoulders, made a face, and then— through the haze of fresh pot smoke and laziness—he said, "I say we take another bong rip, or seven, then start blowing stuff up."

"First off, I like your thinking, but I don't at the same time. What should we blow up?"

"Dude, where's your head?" Chad asked, tapping his skull. "If we blow these things up, they'll explode by themselves. But if we blow up like a car, or a truck, something with a bunch of gas, that'd be way more cool."

"Oh yeah," Wagner said, super baked. "Yeah, I like it. Okay."

"Should we just go now?"

"No way, José," Wagner said, practically smoking down the last millimeter. He inhaled, held it, then squinted his eyes and blew out a less than enthusiastic stream of smoke. "Let's go at night. We can turn the midnight hour into sunrise."

"Man, when you get wasted, you get totally poetic."

Smiling, scratching his head, he said, "It's what I do man. It's what I motherfreaking do."

# CHAPTER EIGHT

The *bang, bang, bang!* of gunshots echoing inside the Walgreen's puts those of us outside on edge. If Rex and Indigo were fired upon, if they were shot and killed, then any minute now the killers might come running out the front door where Stanton can hopefully take them out.

We should be so lucky.

If they don't come running out, and Indigo and Rex don't let us know they're okay, then chances are I'm going to have a mental breakdown right before doing something seriously stupid.

At this point I'm checking myself for heart palpitations, frantic breathing, hyperventilation. My weapon is in my hand, as awkward and as heavy as it is, and it's aimed with Stanton's at the Walgreen's front door.

Macy, for a change, is doing exactly as she's told. She's staying behind us.

Out here with little for cover, the three of us are an ocean of perpetual silence. My worst fears are coming true: nothing's happening. Now I can't stop the tide of potential scenarios from flooding into my mind. I have to know if my little brother is still alive.

The guns get too heavy to hold; we lower them to our sides.

Newly minted vagrants wander by us, looking at us funny, or with dead eyes, then turning their attention to the Walgreen's. They don't stop, though, and they don't talk to us. We don't exactly look like the most sociable bunch.

Then again, the way it was raining sludge earlier, how it's matted in our hair and clumpy on our clothes, you can pretty much assume we all look like hobos who've been asleep in our own filth for way too long.

Then there's that part of me, the nurse side of me, who can't stop obsessing over Stanton's wound. If this crap got in it, if it was packed inside the gash, how long until infection set in? And is there any antiseptic left inside the Walgreen's? Because I'm going to need something to clean it once we find someplace safe to call home.

"What's taking so damn long?" Macy finally asks.

"Language," Stanton says too casually.

"Dad, this is the end of the world, no one gives a crap if I say damn," Macy retorts.

I spin around and say, "I do. And your father does. And if we have any hope of returning to more civil times, it's going to be in our ability to preserve our respectability. So no bad words and no bad behavior."

*Beyond killing people and stealing their homes and holding up a Walgreen's after slaughtering a pack of gangbangers...*

Softly, more reverently, her voice raspy from breathing smoke all day, Macy says, "Do you hear how crazy that sounds right now, Mom?"

"I do," I admit.

"Good manners and civility will get us killed," Macy says in the same scratchy, patient voice, like she's the voice of reason here.

"No it won't," Stanton argues. "Poor judgment will get us killed."

My mind is beginning to spiral. I'm too worried about Rex to just stand here having such a poorly timed, unproductive conversation. If the girl wants to cuss, honestly, it would be a big improvement over murder, justified or otherwise.

"We can't just sit here and wait this out," Macy says, echoing all of our feelings.

I shoot her a cursory look. This whole time we've been outside the Walgreen's, waiting, all I've been doing is thinking about Macy. About how she killed that man. How it was like she didn't even stop to think or hesitate. She just acted.

"Just because you did...what you did back there...to that man, it doesn't mean you're some kind of a badass that can just charge headlong into danger. A loaded gun isn't a get-out-of-death-free card."

Macy reels, makes a face.

"I get that these are different times," I say, "that we're really in a life-and-death situation on the daily, but life still matters. Yours more than all of ours."

"Mom, calm down," Macy says. "We're all still alive, I just want to make sure Uncle Rex is okay."

"He's been to war before, certainly something much worse than this and he's okay, so—"

"You realize he was shot?" Stanton says.

"Dammit, stop. I don't need you taking her side with everything I say—"

He raises his hands in mock surrender and says, "I'm not. It's just...we can't lose our collective ess aych eye tee right now."

"Did you just spell 'shit' in front of our fifteen year old daughter?" I ask him, aghast.

"I know how to spell, Dad."

"She knows how to spell, Stanton."

We fall into one giant, collective brooding spell, one we might not be able to crawl out from. Stanton, sure—he seems to be coping fine. And Macy? She's doing fine for now, too. But me? This is all just a little too much.

"What do we even know about this girl?" I hear myself ask.

"That she's amazing," Macy says.

"Why? Because she can shoot a bow and arrow and she reminds you of that Hunger Games girl?"

"Yeah," Macy says. "Sort of."

"Well this isn't the movies and we're really in trouble here. This isn't a joke. It's not *a situation*. And if you look around, I'm not really sure we'll ever see a fix for this."

There's a low rolling smoke cloud covering the city. It's dark and daunting and settling in like a wet fog. A patch that size is sure to cause more problems in the hours to come, if only in our burning throats and lungs. We have to find some place to stay, and fast.

When no one says anything, I say, "I'm going in."

"No," Stanton says.

"Macy's right, as much as it pains me to say so. We can't just sit out here when they could be dead inside, or bleeding to death."

"I'll go," Stanton offers.

"You're not a nurse."

He falls quiet.

"Just be careful in there," he says, "because if there's any indication of trouble, Macy and I are coming in after you."

"Roger that," I say, starting across the street.

As I'm contemplating my next moves, as I'm assessing the situation with as much awareness and stealth as I can muster, I'm telling myself that Rex is equipped for war, that he understands the intricacies of combat and control and that things are Kosher inside. I'm also thinking about Indigo and feeling like it's clear that she can handle herself, so really I'm just being some kind of a nervous Nelly.

As for yours truly, I can't say anything other than if I die, it'll probably be doing something stupid.

Something just like this.

# CHAPTER NINE

From the muddy, juicy waters of unconsciousness came a pair of bee-sting pains radiating out from the gun shot wounds in his arms. Things cleared, but not much. The only thing changing was the levels of pain. Plus, Rex was having a hard time making connections through the drag and pull he was feeling on his body.

His mind said *gunshot wounds*.

His mind said *war*.

From miles away, he heard the woman sobbing, and the girl fast talking, and then he heard the muffled sounds of shuffling and hitting and a soft yelping. His eyes cracked open, his eyelids heavy, swollen. Bright fluorescent light cut through to his brain making his head hurt. His mouth was making mumbling noises on its own, his body shifting from the pain. Then she was there, in his face: Indigo. There is red splatter on her cheek. Not her blood. Her eyes were wild, but calming for him.

"Oh my gosh, I thought I lost you for a second," she said.

"Really?" he asked from like a million miles away.

"No," she said, sarcastic. "You got shot in the arm. You passed out. Now here you are after all the hard work is done waking up like a newborn after his nap. Perhaps I should check your diaper."

"It's probably dirty."

His head was clearing fast now, so he tried to sit up.

"And here I thought you were the professional," she said.

"I'm a terrible victim."

"Aren't we all," she said, helping him sit up.

The pounding in his head subsided long enough for him to look down and see Indigo's hostage wearing only a pair of panties. She wasn't a pretty sight. The girl was slumped over sideways, but she was turned at the torso and sprawled face-down on the cold industrial floors.

"What did you do to her?" he asked.

The small room was cold, and it smelled of blood, gunpowder residue and cooked meat. In the corner was a small charcoal barbeque grill. There were bottles of water opened nearby and his arm felt stiff. Looking down he saw it was bandaged.

"She wasn't as cooperative as she first led me to believe," Indigo said.

"And the bruises?"

The hostage's back was lined with them, a bunch of fist sized black and blue marks.

"She needed some help remembering some things."

"How bad is it?" he asked.

"You or her?"

"Her. This situation. Whatever this is you got us messed up in."

Indigo's mouth was a flat line, her eyes devoid of any emotion. Her hair was pulled back into a ponytail with more than a few loose strands hanging in her face, but she was just as dirty as everyone else.

"It's bad. Worse than I thought."

"Care to elaborate?" he asked, chewing on the pain and becoming irritated by how cryptic she was being. "I mean, I'd love to have some sort of valid justification for killing that guy, otherwise..."

"I get it. I can only tell you what she told me, and hopefully she isn't lying. She says the Mission District has by far the most dangerous gangs, followed by SoMa."

"SoMa?"

"South of Market."

"Go ahead," he said, looking at the girl, who finally stopped sobbing and was instead reaching for something to cover herself with.

"No!" Indigo barked. The girl pulled back. Then, to Rex, she said, "You've heard of the MS-13, right?"

"Sure."

"Worst gang in America before all this. Imagine a bunch of narcissistic mass murderers on power trips. They have no decency, no respect for life and no respect for age. When they pull you into the fold, you could be ten years old or thirty and it wouldn't matter to them. Basically, from what this nasty slag is telling me, they practically tear your soul from your body as payment."

"Jesus," he muttered.

"Making matters worse, the MS-13 have basically aligned themselves with the Sureños, which is the southern California branch of the Mexican Mafia. Before this they were expanding their territory north at an alarming rate."

"So what does all that have to do with our girl and her dead friends, and the black snakes they have tattooed on their bodies?"

"Everything," she said. "The MS-13 and the Sureños are basically rivals with the Norteños, which is the northern California faction of the Nuestra family. The violence that breaks out between these two warring factions is supposedly a thing of legend, although San Francisco seems to have a way of covering up all its piles of crap with pretty rugs."

Waving off the commentary, he said, "So these gangs, they're what...rivals for The Ophidian Horde?"

"No. The Ophidian Horde is a mop-up gang. The drone attack on the city wasn't about skin color or age. The machines didn't care about race or religion, about gang members or priests. A lot of people died in the attacks. A lot of them leaving their organizations weak and in disarray."

"So this gang, they're trying to organize...all the gangs?" he asked.

"According to this piece of white trash filth, they're not pulling in the Sureños, the Norteños or the MS-13. Not just yet. They're going after the low level gangs like the Knockout Gang, Eddy Rock, the Page Street Mob. They're pulling them all into one organization and telling them they will be the ruling gang once the Sureños and the Norteños get done killing each other."

"So how does any of this effect us directly?"

"They're going to own you," the girl moaned from the floor. She turned her face up to Rex and it was so badly beaten and so filled with rage it made him wince. "They're going to own this town, but not before they kill off all the *pendejos* like you!"

"Is this true?" Rex asked, looking up at Indigo.

Seeing the girl's face beaten so badly made him look at Indigo differently. It made him wonder what the hell really happened to her that she should be like this. Was she was always so violent, so sullen? Or was this merely a reaction to all the bad things that happened to her?

"According to her, yes. But under interrogation, people will sometimes say anything they think you want them to say. That's why we're going to tie her up and leave her here until we can verify her story."

The outrage and the million-miles-an-hour cursing that spewed from this girl's mouth was like nothing Rex had ever heard before. He could see blood vessels popping in the whites of her eyes as she screamed and it sort of scared him. All this *after* she'd been beaten.

Indigo went and cracked her so hard on the top of the skull the raging beast withered, covering her head where it began to bleed and whimpering to herself once more.

"Do you enjoy that?" Rex asked. "Clubbing people over the head with your gun?"

"Actually, no. But desperate times, and all that," she said. "Can you walk?"

"I can," a voice said from behind them. They both turned, but Indigo had her gun aimed at the source of the noise.

Cincinnati.

His sister was armed, too. Cincinnati put both hands out and raised them before her. Indigo immediately lowered her gun and said, "That's a great way to get an extra hole in your face."

Looking down at the mauled and naked girl, she said, "Apparently so. Where are her clothes?"

"Somewhere over there," Indigo said, not looking or motioning anywhere.

"Why are they not on her body?"

"Because if she's telling us the truth, she gets to leave. But she was slow to talk, so I kept taking them away. When she walks, if she's honest with us, the deal was she could leave with only the clothes on her body."

"But she'll freeze to death," Cincinnati said.

"Not my problem."

"What *is* your problem?" Cincinnati finally asked. Rex sensed the agitation in his sister and hoped that it wouldn't screw things up too badly with Indigo.

"My problem is there's about to be a massive turf war between the city's most violent gangs in an attempt to concentrate power. If you think the destruction that's been hitting us so far is bad, it's about to get a whole lot worse."

"I don't understand."

"This girl was just some low level skank for the MS-13 who decided to jump ship and try another gang. Now she's a full blooded member of The Ophidian Horde, and from what she's telling me, this war isn't only going to spill over into the streets and onto normal people, it's going to claim San Francisco as its territory while systematically enslaving the people. Imagine the mob, but with no police. Imagine no law. No one to stop the rapes and the murders; no one to stop men on a mission to control this city. If they get the upper hand, if they get that swing of power, then it's over for us. Unless we can get out."

"We've tried."

"Everyone's tried," Indigo said.

"Perhaps it's time to try again," Rex added.

"Or perhaps this is our home and our city and we shouldn't just sit around like a bunch of pansies talking about running."

"What are you suggesting?" Rex asked Indigo.

"Yeah," Cincinnati said. "What are you suggesting?"

Indigo looked at them both, as serious as Rex had ever seen her, and then she said, "I'm suggesting we stop them before they get started."

There was a lot of silence and some consternating looks followed by the gravely, blood soaked laughter of their prisoner.

"You just go ahead and try," she said, laughing her way into a small crying jag.

"Can I ask you a personal question?" Rex said to Indigo, ignoring the hostage. Indigo folded her arms and pursed her lips. "How big are your balls?"

Blowing out a sigh, but not once blinking or taking her eyes off him, she said, "Big enough to shoot hoops with. Now are we going to find you guys a place to live, or are you going to just sit there and bleed?"

Turning to Cincinnati, who looked like she couldn't believe any of this was happening, he said, "Mark my words, big sis, one day I'm going to have this girl's babies."

Indigo punched him in the shoulder where he was first shot and said, "Not likely," as he let out a yelp and chewed down on the sharp, stabbing pain.

Indigo then grabbed her hostage by the hair and dragged her

kicking and screaming to a chair, not paying attention to the slew of death threats and howling erupting from the girl's mouth.

"Don't look at her tits," Cincinnati said.

"Too late," Rex replied.

"Help me tie her up," Indigo said. Cincinnati handed her gun to Rex, then went to look at the woman's injuries before helping secure her.

"Was all this necessary?" she asked Indigo.

"I wouldn't have done it otherwise."

Cincinnati was studying the blonde girl's forehead, which was bumpy and blue. There were a few cuts on her brows as well, evidence that Indigo's hostage had been struck repeatedly.

"And what about them?" she asked. "The two guys outside with their heads blown wide open? Was that necessary, too?"

"Save me your humanitarian gestures," she said.

"You can't just go around killing people," Cincinnati said.

"Maybe you should have that conversation with your brother. He's been shot again, by the way. Triceps. Passed out like he was new."

His sister drew a deep breath, then let it out in a long exhale. She couldn't even look at him. "Before today, he was new. To getting shot, that is."

"Um...hello. I'm right here," Rex said. "I can hear everything you're saying."

Without looking back at him, Cincinnati said, "Good, then get up and go get Stanton and Macy. Tell them to come in here."

"Why?"

She spun and leveled him with big sister eyes. "To go shopping, Rex. We need supplies in case you forgot."

"We need a house first," Rex grumbled, getting himself off the table.

"I told you I've got you covered there," Indigo said. She was binding the girl's wrists behind her back with a length of rope, then wrapping that same rope around her throat. If she tried to struggle, it looked to Rex like the girl ran the risk of choking herself.

"Can't we at least put a shirt on her?" Rex said.

"You don't like my boobs?" the girl asked, angry, unable to mop up her eyes.

"Sure I do," Rex said. "They look just like my grandma's."

Indigo stopped, shook her head, then went over to a supplies cabinet, pulled out grey duct tape, then came back and wrapped a length of tape across her breasts, covering her nipples. The girl protested mightily, but she only ended up nearly choking herself.

"See?"

Rex turned and left. He found both Stanton and Macy creeping in the front door. Stanton saw him, stood up straight and appeared to relax.

"You okay?"

"Not really," Rex said. "Grab a cart, we're going shopping. Oh, and watch out for the poop over there by the dead guy. I'm pretty sure it's human."

# CHAPTER TEN

We're rolling an old shopping cart packed to the hilt with stuff from Walgreen's down this dirt alley Indigo says is really called Dirt Alley.

Apparently this is how you go house shopping in the apocalypse.

The cart's jacked up wheels aren't exactly quiet, but Indigo says she can both shoot arrows and show houses at the same time. It's kind of nice to have a defender on our side. Already I'm feeling better about her. More optimistic.

So Indigo is pointing to this house and that, telling us about floor plans and lighting and which homes seem to have the nicest stuff. It's crazy to think that less than an hour ago she killed some people and beat some pretty important information out of a member of the gang poised to take over the city now that it had no law or military presence.

"I want my own room," Macy says.

"Naturally," Indigo replies with a jovial smile.

"How do you know all about these houses?" Macy asks. "Were they the homes of friends of yours?"

Indigo doesn't speak, she just bites her lip and keeps walking.

"She knows them because she's looted them," Stanton finally

says. "Not that I blame her. She was just being resourceful, and in this world, what you do to survive seems to trump how bad you look and feel for robbing abandoned homes in a collapsed society."

"It's survival of the fittest," Indigo says. "That one over there belonged to a friend of mine, so you can't stay there. Watch the pile of ash. You'll trip over the bones if you're not careful."

We make a wide berth around a huge ash pit full of bones and belt buckles and several skulls. My God, these are human bones! What the hell?

"Whose ash pit is that?" I ask, trying to keep the anxiety out of my voice.

"Mine," she says. "I made it."

"What was it you burned in there?" I ask. "And why can't we stay in your friend's house?"

"The ash pit contains the first members of The Ophidian Horde when they came here and tried to kill me and my friend. And you can't stay in my friend's house because she's still there."

"What's her name?" Macy asks.

"Dead."

No one says anything. It gets terribly uncomfortable for a second.

"And she's still there?" Stanton chimes in.

At a small detached garage, Indigo leans down and lifts the garage door. Inside is an old black and gold muscle car with a front end that's seen better days.

There are also supplies.

And weapons.

"Take two cases of water and that bucket there"—she says pointing to the corner of the garage—"and you can pick that house there and there if you want to stay where I can keep an eye on you." She's now pointing to the houses on either side of her friend's house. "Both homes are nice and there's plenty of room for all of you."

"Will I get my own room?" Macy asks.

"Yes. Plus both homes still have water in the water heaters. Conserve where you can though, because when we're out, we're going to be hauling in water from other houses, nearby water holes and eventually the bay. When we have to do that, the process by which to leech the salt out is slow and tedious and not anything I'm looking forward to."

"Why can't we stay with you?" Rex asks.

"Because I have company."

"A boyfriend?" Macy asks with a knowing grin.

"Something like that. Besides, I figure we don't even know each other, so it's too soon to start sleeping together."

"I'm okay with it if you are," Rex says, cradling his injured arm.

"I'm not," Indigo replies, not the least bit humored. Ignoring Rex's antics, looking first at Macy, then at me, she says, "At least not yet. It's a trust thing, really. Plus some really bad things have happened and my guest was privy to them. She had a front row seat, unfortunately, and I'm not inclined to overwhelm her with company."

"Flashlight?" Stanton asks looking around.

She hands him two flashlights and says, "I've got batteries when you run out, but as with everything...conserve."

"Sure thing," Rex says.

"You guys can settle in tonight and tomorrow, but the day after that we need to pow-wow and figure this thing out. There's no freeloaders allowed in this new world," Indigo says, now looking directly at Rex, "even if you've been shot. Twice. You have to pull your own weight and then some."

"We will," I say.

"You?" Indigo says, looking at me, "I don't doubt. But him..."

"You're worried about me?" Rex asks.

"Yes."

Nodding his head, shrugging off the comment, he says, "I'll be fine. Thanks for the concern, though."

"I appreciate you having my back in there," she grumbles.

Smiling but moving gingerly, Rex says, "Let's go guys. I'm in favor of the house on the right, all agreed say 'aye.'"

"We're going to the other house," Macy says. Stanton and I agree. "It just looks cleaner."

"And bigger," Indigo says. They all look at her one last time. Then: "In time perhaps I'll invite you over, but for now—especially you, Rex—don't get any funny ideas. Anyone who comes into my house without an invitation takes a round to the face."

Stanton, Macy and I turn to Rex who says, "I'm a fighter not a lover."

And that's that.

"Oh, before I forget," Indigo says. She heads inside, then comes back out a few minutes later and hands me a small bottle of hydrogen peroxide and a suturing kit, complete with the needle and thirty six inches of absorbable suture. "The hydrogen peroxide is for Stanton's head, but the stitches are for Rex's mouth." She says this and doesn't smile. She just looks at Rex with even, no-nonsense eyes.

"Thank you," I tell her, deeply grateful, even if she is making us all a bit uncomfortable.

We say good-bye to Indigo and head to the house Rex didn't choose. If he complains, I'll tell him he can stay there if he wants, but he doesn't complain.

As we're heading back across the way, we make a wide berth around the pile of bones and head through a collapsed section of wood fence leading to the house adjacent to Indigo's backyard.

"Mom," Macy says. "When I grow up I want to be like Indigo."

"Me, too," I hear myself mumble

———

"I don't know about this," Macy says. The house feels like a tomb. Cold, dark, empty. It's a house though, and it doesn't smell like death, rotten food or mold, so that's a plus.

"Should've gone with the other house," Rex says.

I head around and open the windows, drenching the space in light. The hardwood floors are new, but covered in old rugs, the furniture old but polished to a light shine.

"All it needed was some light," I say.

Sniffing around the first floor rooms gives me nothing of interest. Meaning no one's died in here yet. There isn't old food or dirty plates stacked in the sink, no spoiled milk in the fridge (yet) because it's a bit barren in there, and the shopping list stuck to the fridge has lots of items on it which tells me this person was clean and responsible, but not rolling in the money.

"They cared about their home," Stanton says.

"Yeah," I hear myself say.

Macy heads upstairs with Rex to find their respective bedrooms. I'm praying they realize that no matter what, Stanton and I will be taking the master.

Or maybe not.

I'm just happy my boys are still alive, and I'm happy my husband and I are still together. That all of us are together.

Looking out into the backyard, my eyes go to the half-kicked over fence, then to the yard itself, which is mostly dirt and some stacked up garbage along the fence line. It's not the best view, but it isn't terrible either.

"It's less nice than I thought," Stanton says, "but with some grow boxes, some clean dirt and some seeds, we might be able to plant."

"That's a bit optimistic," I say, not meaning to be a buzzkill, but realizing I am anyway. Looking up I say, "Sorry. It's just... there's so much more that has to come before that."

"I know. No sense in being like you though. Pessimism never was my strong suit."

I turn and pull him into an easy hug, burying my face in his neck and telling him how much I love him. He holds me for like forever, and I just want to stay here—in his arms—until our final days, may they not come too soon.

"I miss you," he says.

"I miss you, too," I tell him.

It feels like it's been forever since we've held each other like this. It's almost like our bodies understand this and won't let go. Then he steps away, leans forward and kisses me on the mouth and I swear it's like something in my chest opens up again and I can breathe.

When our mouths come apart, I say, "Let me clean your cut, see if we need stitches."

We head upstairs where there is a long hallway and three bedrooms. Rex and Macy are in rooms next to each other and we're at the end of the hall. In the master.

I pop my head in Macy's bedroom and she's stretched out on a full-sized bed that's taking up most of the space. There are posters of Japanese anime and a *Fight Club* poster, and the bed is gender neutral with stuffed animals that could either be for a boy or a girl. There's also a small desk with papers and pencils out, and a Captain America action figure. It's cute.

"You're going to get the bed dirty," I say, thinking about the comforter.

"It's like being on clouds, Mom!" she replies.

"Pretty soon those clouds will just be pillows of dust if you're not careful."

Spinning over and burying her face in the sheets, she says, "They smell like summertime."

Smiling, happy she's no longer forced to sleep on a couch, I leave her to her room. Rex is further down the hall, at the end of the house where there's a window facing Dirt Alley, and Indigo's home. He's standing at the window, his body relaxed but his mind working overtime for sure.

"Stalker to the end," I say.

He doesn't even flinch at the sound of my voice, at the subtle suggestion, or offense, depending on how he looks at it.

"If you were a guy," he asks, not even turning around, "wouldn't you be, too?"

I think about it and it doesn't take long for me to answer.

"I suppose so."

"Do you think I should be embarrassed for passing out after getting shot? I mean, is that normal?"

"Yes, and no. Well, maybe sometimes."

He gives a defeated laugh that's tortured by longing, or perhaps fatigue. He then turns around with this wondrous light in his eyes and says, "The way she just went to work on those guys, like it didn't affect her one bit—and how she interrogated the blonde at Walgreen's—it's like we were two halves of a whole with perfect lines between us. Like we fit. Like she was that missing thing I didn't know I wanted until I saw her in action and decided she was the one."

"Little brother," I hear myself saying, sad, careful not to wipe my feet on the platitudes of his mind, "you're always falling in love with the wrong girls at the wrong time."

His eyes clear, like his trance is momentarily broken. He licks his lips and says, "I saw a lot of terrible things overseas. We did some...some bad things." He just stands there, silent and unmoving, the memories in his head having their way with him. "You can't love anything over there. You don't want to."

I want to cross the room, wrap my arms around him. It's not the right time, though. Whatever his brain is pulling from the past, however horrifying the memories might be, I've been around him long enough to let him be in them. His therapist said he needs to stay in them to be able to understand them, and to eventually let them go.

"So when I get back to the states," he says, "and I see all these beautiful people just living their lives, not trying to kill you, not plotting to kill each other, I think that maybe it's okay to relax, to put my guard down, and so I do just that."

His eyes start to water, his features bending to the horrors. He's looking at me, seeing me, yet that's not exactly true. His eyes aren't even focused. All he can see are the times and places that ruined him, and all those little traumas he can't quite bury.

Then something shifts and he begins to speak. "The second I let my guard down and kept it down, I began to see things differently, all the love that refused to...to...it just comes flooding forth at once. It's honestly...a bit overpowering."

The tears drip over and now I can see he's seeing me. He wipes his eyes as the memories become physical pain.

Now it's time.

Walking to him, pulling him into the safety of my arms, I tell him the things he needs to hear. "You're not safe here, but you're loved. You won't ever forget those memories, because you can't, because you won't, but you'll make new ones. Maybe they'll be with us, maybe they will be with other people. But they'll be new."

"I like Indigo," he says, sniffling.

"We all sort of do, but she's just a girl we didn't know a few hours ago. She's cute, good with a bow and her girl balls are gigantic, but she's damaged, Rex. Something's not quite right about her."

"She's damaged like me," he whispers.

"Yes."

"That could be a good thing, right?" he asks with hopeful eyes. "I mean, we could relate to each other about...you know, the stuff in our lives that happened to us. The stuff we've done."

"It could be the perfect match, or it could be dysfunctional to the point of catastrophic. People who have too much in common, especially when it comes to surviving traumatic events, sometimes they can either heal each other or end up wrecking each other."

He moves away from me, fixes himself and says, "You're right. It's best not to take a chance."

"There are no absolutes," I tell him, leaving room for hope.

He doesn't run with it. Instead, he turns and pulls the drapes shut and says, "You're right. Best to just forget about her."

"How bad do you think this thing is," I ask, changing subjects.

"Bad," he says, his voice flat, completely devoid of emotion. He starts to take off his boots. His socks are in good shape, but one of them has a small hole in the heel that's bound to get a lot bigger depending on how much walking we're going to be doing in the days ahead.

"Do you think there's a fix?"

"A nuclear EMP isn't a temporary situation," he says. He wipes his eyes. He's almost back to normal. "It basically fries the grid and just about anything with a computer chip in it."

"Pretty much everything has a chip in it these days."

"Exactly."

He pulls off his shirt and I turn because I can't look at all the scars. It only serves to remind me of what happened to him. How he was taken hostage and beaten daily to within an inch of his life.

"I should really look at your head."

"I've been feeling it and it's mostly just a knot," he says. "It won't need stitches."

"I should really clean it and see for myself," I tell him.

"When you're ready."

A few minutes later I return. He's laying in bed with the covers over him and his clothes folded in a neat stack on the floor. His shoes are placed beside them, neat, organized.

I take a look at where the thugs from the field hit him and it's indeed a pretty nasty knot. But the cut isn't deep or wide. I wipe the affected area with a damp cloth, dry it, then spritz the wound with the little brown bottle of hydrogen peroxide Indigo gave me.

I know it stings, but he doesn't move.

Blowing on it will help, but he won't speak to that either. The clear liquid mixes with a bit of blood and I dab the pink tears it's making with a square of gauze from the suture kit. On closer inspection, the cut seems to be doing fine.

It just needs to breathe.

I lean forward, kiss the top of his head, then give the wound a hearty smack because that's how they do it in the military. He grabs his head and fires me a look.

"Love you little brother."

"Love you too, Sis."

———————

Stanton is waiting for me when I get in the room. Immediately I walk into a space darkened by blackout drapes that are pulled shut. There is a flickering of light though, from a pair of candles burning on the night stands flanking the queen sized bed. There's plenty of daylight outside, but in here, there's only mood lighting. My mind is suddenly divided between this hell we're doing our damnedest to survive and a romantic interlude with my husband—something neither of us have seen in the better part of a year.

"What's this?" I ask.

I'm thinking maybe he hit his head a little harder than I realized if what he's trying to do in the apocalypse is get laid. He hasn't really been himself, though, not since the old lady. Perhaps he's finally pulling out of it. Perhaps this will help.

Stanton is sitting in bed. Beside the bed is a pile of his dirty clothes. With an anticipatory look on his face, one side of the bed's comforters are pulled open like an invitation.

"Lock the door," he says.

I do.

"Take off your clothes," he says.

I take them off, not too slowly, but not in a rush either.

"I'm filthy," I say, feeling the gunk in my hair, the dryness of my skin, specifically around my eyes and across my forehead.

"That's the girl I know and love," he says with a grin.

"No, I mean like, I'm dirty."

"So we'll have dirty sex and then we'll wash each other later. I have two bottles of water with your name on them."

Yeah, I think with a grin, my husband is coming back.

"Did you save one for yourself?" I ask, playful.

"I did."

He pats the bed, telling me to come.

As exhausted as I am, as overwhelmed as this day has left me —as these last weeks have left me—I see the man I fell in love with and I don't want him to go away again.

So I go to him.

I slide into a the bed where the sheets are cool, but luxurious and soft. The soft cooing that escapes me is the linen's doing, and the mattress's doing. But after that, all the little noises I make, all the powerful exultations, that's purely Stanton's doing.

When we're done, we just hold each other until it's time to bathe and maybe try to find something to eat.

Stanton washes me in the tub; I wash him as well. We dry each other off, then try to find some clothes in a closet that's not ours. There are clothes that are clean, but they're a bit big. Whatever. We don't care. At least *I* don't care. There was no way I was getting back into the heap of an outfit I left on the floor beside the bed.

Downstairs, we all meet for an early dinner. It's tuna and soda crackers. It's warm Sprite with a freshly opened pack of Oreo's for dessert.

We don't say much, other than Macy telling us she loves her room and Rex asking if there are more clean clothes where ours came from.

"Of course," Stanton says.

"Go pick out an outfit, if you want," I tell Rex. He seems a bit down, but that's because he's still brooding over deciding to let Indigo go.

He'll see her again, though, and maybe he'll go back to trying to get her, or perhaps he's not going to engage in the chase. Either way, this side of Rex is as hard to watch as the side of him that's overly optimistic.

That night I have a hard time sleeping. It's too quiet. For the last few weeks I've loved the quiet, but only because this soft reverence, this burst of peacefulness, was what followed the bombing runs that had been going on all day long almost non-stop.

Now it's only stillness, and silence.

It's too eerie.

"What do you think we should do with this world?" I ask Stanton in the dark. It must be nearly ten when I ask this.

He mumbles something, then rolls over taking a bit of the covers with him. His head wound wasn't as bad as I thought it would be, but it did require stitches. I touch the area around the wound, the area I cleaned and stitched up. Laying my hand flat on this head, I move my fingers into his hair.

"I think we should try to restore it," I say.

"Me, too," he says, groggy.

He probably won't even remember this conversation, and I won't blame him. I kind of want to do something for this city. Try to put it back together. Try to make it my home despite the many dangers of living here. But not tonight.

That will be tomorrow.

In the morning, we'll figure out what to do, how to survive in this place. And if we can do that without killing anyone, well then, that will just be fantabulous.

# CHAPTER ELEVEN

It was time. Outside, the sun was setting and already the temperature dropped a few degrees. Rider checked his hair, his teeth and his weapon, and then he took a deep breath and walked down the hall to Sarah's room.

At her door, he knocked lightly. She opened it a minute later and he drew an involuntary breath.

"Yes?" she asked, clearly pleased by his reaction.

"Wow." He froze, then realized what he was doing. He was staring. "I mean, you look nice, Doc."

"Sarah," she said.

She wore a knit hat pulled loosely on a head of sandy brown hair, an attractive mid-length coat, tight jeans and ankle boots. This wasn't exactly walking wear, but she was just about as beautiful as he'd ever seen.

He smiled, reached for her hand. She took it, closing and locking the door behind her. It was strange holding her hand, but he wanted to and she didn't grow tense under his grip. He looked at her as they strolled through the dimly lit halls, then she looked up at him and said, "I like the way you look, too, Rider. How are your wounds?"

"They feel amazing," he replied with a grin.

"There's something about a tough guy I find...curious."

"I'm not a tough guy," he said. "Just someone trying to survive this mess long enough to see what's on the other side."

When they arrived at the door leading outside, Rider opened it, held it for her. He didn't care what anyone said, chivalry wasn't dead. At least, it wasn't dying on his watch.

"Thank you."

Outside, she took his hand this time, which thrilled him. He didn't realize just how alone he felt until he found himself in the casual company of a new woman. Looking at her in the setting sun, a burning glow in the smoky eastern skies, he realized he was inexplicably drawn to her.

"What if there's nothing on the other side of this?" she asked. "What if this is it?"

He stayed with this thought for a minute. He'd been wondering the same thing, especially after the lights went out and the power died. The EMP strike sacrificed the grid to take out the immediate threat. Did they have a new plan for restoring power, or was this simply a reactionary strike?

He assumed he already knew the answer. He could be wrong, though. He'd been wrong before and he'd certainly be wrong again.

"I guess we make do with what we have," he said, the pain in his leg trying to get the best of him.

"Just like that?"

"I spent some time in country," he said.

"Which country?"

"Not this one," he replied. "You can't predict what's going to happen when you're deep in enemy territory, or caught in a fire-fight with no way out. You just look around and make do with what you have. The guy next to you gets shot, you tell yourself he's the lucky one, and then you dig in. You get captured, or shot, or trapped, you dig in long enough and hard enough to find an exit."

"Did you always find an exit?"

This question spurred so many memories. When they were in the field, if they didn't have a way out, more often than not they made one. They went through a door, a person, a village. If they didn't have an escape route, they kicked a hole in whatever stood in their way knowing they were on their own and that the US government would disavow them if they were caught.

"Yes," he answered, "we always found an exit."

"Do you see one here?"

He held her eye and said, "Yes."

"Where?"

They came up on one of the two guard posts, which was just a guy in the back of another truck with weapons enough to handle a small army.

"Evening," the guard said with a subtle nod. He acknowledged Rider, but his eyes went directly to Sarah.

Rider thought the watchman's name was Sal, but he couldn't be sure. "How is it out there?"

Barely tearing his eyes off Sarah, he said, "Quiet."

"On the street?"

The guy nodded and said, "On the street and in the air. You armed?"

"Of course," he said.

They didn't know each other yet, because the group inside the college was growing well into the dozens and he wasn't the social type, but there would be plenty of time in the future to remedy that. Still, he didn't have to stare. Then again, the man had a sturdy look about him. Like he had no problem going to knuckles in a tussle. So maybe he looked at Sarah a bit too long, and maybe he liked what he saw.

Rider smiled, didn't blame the guy. The penance for dating a good looking woman was that other men would always see in her what he'd first seen. She was beautiful. So beautiful and young to the world, in fact, that girls with looks and a body like hers would always draw the eye of many an aggressive man.

"Sarah," the guard said with a polite nod.

"Sal," she answered with a grin.

Rider pumped her hand lightly, prompting her to look at him. With bright eyes and an ease about her, she said, "Lead the way."

"Be careful out there," Sal warned. "Things can turn on a dime."

"Don't I know it," Rider said.

Sarah and Rider walked up Ashbury Street, marveling at the canopy of telephone wires and the three and four story homes that looked like they all had a fresh face lift before this.

Rider was intensely aware of her, of her smells, the feel of her, how her hair was long and straight and he wanted to touch it, to brush it back from her face ear so he could better see her features—

Sarah turned and softened her eyes at him, and for the briefest moment, he realized she saw him. She saw his expression and she knew...

"What are you thinking about?" she asked.

"Oh, this and that," he said, playing coy.

Her mouth curled into a delighted smile, highlighting a small pair of dimples he'd seen before and found adorable. She seemed to be enjoying herself. On the other hand, he felt more at ease being shot at than being with her. His head was a million unanswered questions. Questions like: *does she like me? Can I be with this girl despite the age gap? What if she's not interested?* Things like that, things that might never have answers, but would persist anytime he was in her company.

"I know that," she said. "I was wondering what *specifically* you were thinking."

"Oh."

Swallowing the lump in his throat, he reached out and brushed a strand of hair back from her cheek, just as he imagined, then said, "I was thinking about how beautiful you look in this light."

She tucked her chin, an unguarded smile coming...a smile of satisfaction, one of enchantment.

"Do you think this is happening in other places, too?" she asked, her voice a little more timid, but not in a bad way. "All this...destruction by the drones? The loss of power?"

"I liked talking about us better," he said. "But yes. I think it's happened elsewhere."

"Is that your instincts talking, or do you know something?"

"If I leaned in and kissed you, would you pull away?" he asked. He didn't mean to ask the question, but he had to. He had to know.

She stopped, let go of his hand and turned to face him. "Is that what you want?"

"Yes."

"Then no, I won't stop you."

And with that, he leaned in and kissed her. Her hand came to his face as their lips touched, and though it wasn't a hungry encounter—because the night and the circumstances didn't warrant that—it was probably the best kiss of his life.

When he pulled away, he drew a deep, satisfied breath and said, "Wow."

"Yeah," she replied, looking down.

He took her hand again and said, "You asked me if I see an exit here, and the answer is yes, but it's not what you think."

"Oh, yeah?" she asked, sounding breathless and a bit whimsical.

"This. You and me. What we did, what we're doing. This is our exit. Our way out of the apocalypse."

"So kissing? That's your big plan?"

He laughed, then looked at her and said, "It's more than that. I'm talking about the human experience. Before all this, we started out working hard to make something of ourselves. In my case I chose to defend the nation against enemies foreign and domestic. In your case, I would think you wanted to help people, yes?"

"Yes."

"But then we went and ruined ourselves with real life. We saw too many horrors, or we felt cut short or abandoned by our employers, or we over-consumed, which is hard to do in a consumer society as healthy as ours. Either way, we created all our little disconnections. We stopped seeing the beauty of family, friends, lovers. It became more about paying the bills, stacking up a pension—"

"Getting through med school."

"Exactly."

"What was the last relationship you were in?" she asked.

"It's been a while," he said.

"Me, too."

"Life can't just be about things. Buying them, collecting them, paying for them. That kiss, our connection, it was amazing...it was the first time I felt...*anything*...in years."

"Really?" she said with a girlish giggle.

"Yeah. It happened in the middle of all this, and yet it felt like the most beautiful thing ever. That's our exit. Not a cleaned up world, or restored order, or even power or running water. Our exit is each other, who we are, how we come together."

In the dying light of the day, a lone gunman walked out of a building where Ashbury dead ended into Fulton. He saw them then stopped. He had a hunting rifle with a scope on it and a tension about him Rider found alarming. He turned and aimed the rifle at Rider, then at Sarah. Rider tensed, stepped back and pulled Sarah behind him. The rifle inched back at Rider. He held his breath.

But the man didn't shoot.

Rider slowly gave a subtle wave of acknowledgement, but the gun still didn't go down. Until it did. The man hurried off into another building and they found they could breathe again.

"I think I might have just wet myself," she said, more serious than not.

"Yeah, that was strange."

"Want to head back?" she asked.

"I do."

When they got back to the compound, the sun had already dropped and she was shivering from the onset of a stiff evening chill. As for himself, Rider could no longer mask the pain in his leg. He was limping a bit at this point.

"It's been cold at night lately," she said.

"No heat will do that."

"I don't have enough blankets, but I don't want anyone else to go without," she said, not looking directly at him, but completely aware of him.

"I have an extra one," he said.

"Perhaps we could combine them," she replied, now looking right at him, a hopeful, expectant look in her eye. "You could keep me safe, and warm, and I could give you your exit."

"I'd like that," he said.

---

The last thing he ever thought he'd have to think about in the apocalypse was falling in love. No one ever really said the words *romance* and *post-apocalyptic nightmare* in the same sentence with a straight face.

It could happen though, couldn't it?

Statistically no one wanted to talk about soul mates and long days in bed eating strawberries and watching chick-flicks and dreaming about happily ever after while outside the pavement was painted red with some dead guy's face, and in the houses all around him everything was rotting fruit, spoiled cream and unflushed toilets.

But Rider would be damned if something new wasn't kicking around in that battered old heart of his.

He'd dragged a blanket and a pillow to her room from his and at first they climbed into bed and cuddled in the dark until she said, "We can produce more body heat together if we're not wearing clothes."

He could have said something clever, but the world was turned upside down and shaken loose and they could all be dead next week, or tomorrow, so instead of being witty or astute, he simply began removing his clothes.

From there he forgot all about the end of civilization as he knew it and lost himself in her body, her touch, in her kiss.

When a guy finds the right girl, nine times out of ten, she's just good in bed and he might not have been laid in awhile. It was easy to mistake good sex with true love. Rider knew he shouldn't do that, but he understood the charm of a fresh face, a new body, open intimacy. She was young, but she didn't come off like it, and they'd had time to build their attraction to each other over the last weeks, which might have solidified what had become a mighty lust for her. So maybe it *was* perfect.

Maybe it had all the necessary ingredients of true love.

Or maybe she'd die tomorrow and it will have just been sex this one time at the front of the end of time.

"What are you thinking about now?" Sarah asked him, running her fingers through his hair.

"I'm thinking about the odds of something like you and me," he said.

"What do you mean?" she asked, scooting closer to him, pressing her breasts into his side.

He was silent for a few moments, gathering his thoughts, trying to think of a way to say it that wouldn't be off-putting or sound like rambling.

"When you go to war, you set aside the notion that you're doing a bad thing. But war is a bad thing. Waging war, as I've come to learn, is more often than not a privilege of the elite. Us career guys think of it as protecting our country from foreign enemies, but the reality is it's almost always about consolidation of both money and power. Then, when it's over, and the rich got fat and well fed, guys like me are left with the nightmares in our head, with the battle scars, with the impossible weight of what we've done."

"Is that why you go on walks?" she asked. "Why you keep to yourself and seem almost shy?"

"Mostly."

"I hope this isn't too forward, but have you had a relationship with a woman since you've been back?"

"One or two, nothing serious."

"Your fault or theirs?" she asked.

He turned and looked at her in the dark, saw the faint outline of her face, and said, "Never mine. I'm amazing."

She laughed at the joke.

"Sometimes when something runs its course," he said, his voice striking a more serious tenor, "two people can walk away from each other and not feel scorned, or resentful, or even broken-hearted. They were like that."

"What war did you fight in?" she asked, easing her leg over his, moving her body even closer to his.

"At some point in time I lost count."

"There was only really one or two right?"

"America is always at war with someone or something, so much so that when you're an operator like I was, you see only missions. Not wars to be won or lost."

"So did you see much combat?" she asked, kissing his neck, his cheek, his earlobe.

"Fortunately and unfortunately."

"And did you have to kill people?" she said, taking hold of him and moving her body onto his once more.

"As much as I appreciate—"

And with that she took him away from his past for a few moments, this time wearing him out damn near completely. When they were done with round two, and the silly notion of falling in love in the apocalypse no longer seemed so trivial— that it might even be a real possibility—he said, "Tell me one thing you've never told anyone else, something that would give me some deeper insight into the world of Sarah Richards."

"What if I can't name that one thing?" she asked, laying on her back, the blankets half off her, her body warm and flush beside him.

"So are you an open book?"

"Only when I trust someone, and then yes, I like to share. Can I trust you, Rider?"

"That's something you'll have to decide on your own, but I'll tell you this, I won't lie to you, deceive you or hurt you."

She laced her fingers in his, laid there for awhile, and then she said, "I once put eye drops in my step-father's coffee and he had explosive diarrhea for two full days. I never told anyone that."

Rider laughed, barely able to picture that. "Why in the world would you do that?"

"I heard him call my mother a bitch with bitch children. I lived with my mom and younger sister at the time. My father left us a few years earlier for another woman. She was apparently pregnant and he claimed he needed to take responsibility for his actions, so he went and made a new family. I guess I just didn't want another deadbeat dad around to break our hearts twice."

"So poisoning him was the solution?" he asked with laughter in his voice.

"It worked," she replied.

"Is your family here with you? I mean, are they here in the compound?"

"My sister died when her high school was bombed and I found my mother's car near her work, burnt to a crisp. She was in the front seat. She tried to call me..."

She stopped speaking, her voice catching. He put his hand upon her face, cupped her cheek as the warm liquid ran from her eyes.

"Why's all this happening?" she asked with a heaviness in her voice.

He rolled over and held her body tight, giving her no explanation, just the love she needed right then. In his arms, she felt so small, so fragile, so...broken.

Like him.

"My brother was in Afghanistan fighting the Taliban when he took friendly fire in the head and neck. He died instantly."

"You mean someone from our side shot him?" she said, sniffling.

He nodded.

"They guarantee it was an accident, but a lot of those guys over there, they're high strung, scared, they make mistakes, or stage accidental friendly fires. I'll never know."

"Accidental friendly fires?" she asked. "Is that even a thing?"

"You remember Pat Tillman?"

"Vaguely."

"NFL player joined the Army out of his patriotic duty, then went over to Afghanistan and began to see the BS of it all. He started to speak out, and it pissed off enough people that when the opportunity struck, a few of his fellow soldiers basically gunned him down. They chalked it up to 'friendly fire.'"

"That's horrible."

"Whether or not that's the absolute truth, friendly fire happens, sometimes on purpose."

"I'm sorry your brother died."

"Me, too. I miss him every day. I was dug in to an op when he passed, so I wasn't ever able to go to his funeral."

"You never really got a chance to say good-bye," she whispered.

"No. But neither did you. And for that, I'm sorry."

As he lay there in her arms, with her warm, soft body resting beside his, a well of emotion flooded forth. He squashed it down. It wouldn't stay buried, though. One day defined so many others, and he couldn't get the memories out of his head.

How had his life come to this? How had he been so bad?

He once killed seven men who thought it would be fun to

torment a group of kids. Visions of him beating these cowards to death unfolded in his mind, stamping out the feelings of loss he suffered thinking about his brother. Unfortunately, these horrors playing in his head also kept him from feeling everything he should be feeling about Sarah.

He didn't know how to deal with all the death he caused. He knew that now. His answer early on was to kill enough people to crush those memories down, to beat the feeling out of his head and heart. It didn't work. But even now, he kept trying, futile as it seemed.

Sarah moved against him, kissed him.

"I feel so alone, Rider," she said. "I know we've only just met, and you're way too old for me, but there's something honest in you, some sad, wholesome part of you that understands what I'm going through, but from a different level. For whatever reason, it makes me feel...not so alone."

"I know you said I'm way too old for you, but did you ever think you're way too young for me?"

Smiling in the dark, she said, "Of course not."

He laughed, and it was the first jovial laugh he'd had in years. Perhaps the hard shell he'd constructed so thoroughly around his heart wasn't so impenetrable.

"So what are you saying?" he asked, hoping she was saying what he *hoped* she was saying.

"I'm saying, you're pretty hot for an old fart, and you can protect us if things turn ugly, which I'm smart enough to know they will. Plus I see the way you look at me. I know that feeling. I have it when I look at you, too."

She was right, he thought. Perceptive and right. The fact that she was feeling the same about him was not only unexpected, but welcome.

If they were ever going to beat back the darkness and hope-lessness this attack had left behind on the city and its people, it would be through moments like this with people like Sarah.

Would he still have to face all these demons though? Would

he still want to hurt those who hurt others to make up for the part of him that lamented his brother's death, and his own run of misdeeds? If so, in this city that once embraced nearly a million souls, there would be gangs, felons, power trippers and monsters.

Plenty of people meant plenty of trouble. And in times like these, the lawless, the cruel and the insane came out from the darkness and into the light. If he could put all his pain into ending their lives, then perhaps he could find meaning again. If he could dispense of it on others, maybe it wouldn't leak out on Sarah, as had happened in all his other relationships.

Or maybe he was still an old, ruined fool.

Feeling her naked body curled against his, he brushed a strand of hair from her head and wondered how long it would be before he broke her heart, before she gave up looking for that something inside of him that had long ago been hollowed out.

# CHAPTER TWELVE

Chad and Wagner set out into the night with their stack of bombs, their last baggie of weed, their papers and their lighter. They were already tripping, but not enough to concern them.

"There's a lot of cars out here," Chad says.

Wagner simply nodded.

"We should go a few blocks up, try out these things in a neighborhood that isn't ours," Chad said.

Wagner just nodded again.

"You okay?"

"I feel...I feel...do you feel it?" he asked, practically dazed. It's dark outside and they were just walking down the street, away from their home.

"Mine's wearing off." His high. That soft, fuzzy edge of everything.

"Yeah, man."

"Let's head up into Presidio Heights," Chad said. That's where they were heading, but someone needed to say it. "Most of that neighborhood is vacant anyway."

"How do you know?" Wagner asked.

"Is it cold out here, or is it just me?"

"Where's your jacket?" Wagner said, looking up at his friend.

Chad's eyes were dropped down on the pipe bombs he was carrying in a box in his arms. Inside the box was his jacket.

"It's keeping the bombs warm," Chad said.

"If they get cold will they blow up?" Wagner asked.

"Of course, that's why we have the jacket."

Wagner rolled his eyes and said, "Dude, you're dumb. Seriously. When did you ever see anything blow up because the conditions were too cold?"

"I may be dumb," Chad said, "but you're still high, so maybe we're both stupid."

At that, they both started laughing, then began talking about how to daisy chain a bunch of the pipe bombs together if they could only find a pair of cars close by.

"First things first," Wagner said, "we try one and go from there."

They walked for the next few blocks in the cold, quiet night, then Chad handed the box to Wagner and said, "This is getting too heavy. You carry it for awhile."

"We're far enough from home," Wagner said.

They looked down one street, then the other, and there they found an older Suburban SUV parked bumper to bumper with a newer Maxima.

"Bingo freaking bango," Chad said.

"Daisy chain?" Wagner asked, his high winding down.

"Hells to the yes."

# CHAPTER THIRTEEN

Sometime in the middle of the night, a bomb exploded so close it shook the entire house. Lenna Justus sat up fast in bed. A hard sleep clung to her, dragging her down when instinct alone had her disoriented, scared and blasted through with a surge of fight-or-flight adrenaline.

Through a fog of delirium, her first concern was for the boys.

Scrambling out of the sheets, she raced from her bedroom down the hallway, nearly slipping on the polished hardwood floor. The boys' door was blown wide open. It looked like Hell had opened a portal and she was staring into its yawning mouth. In that split second, Lenna found herself in the heart of every parent's worst nightmare.

*Are my children alive?*

Stepping inside the bedroom, a quick look left and she was staring at the gaping hole where a wall and a window used to be. The smoking ruin of a sagging roofline was all that was left. Down at the curb, an exploded SUV was in flames alongside the neighbor's Maxima.

Debris littered the boys' bedroom: broken two by fours, glass shards, drywall chunks and powder, smoldering clothes. Outside, firelight illuminated the neighborhood—a lurid sight if ever there was one. Turning away, her eyes frantically zeroed in on the beds.

Both were empty.

"Boys?" she said, tentative, scared of hearing nothing in return. She wanted to scream their names, had intended to, but the lump in her throat was the size of a fist.

Nothing.

Were her boys dead? *Don't think like that!* she screamed inside her head. Hagan, Ballard. Seventeen and fourteen. Gone.

*No!*

Desperate to find them, she tore back the mess of blankets. That's when she found them. They were in a tangle together on the floor, stuffed between the two beds and the wall. Both lay at odd angles, eyes shut, unmoving.

"No, no, no, no, no..." she whimpered frantically.

Neither seemed responsive to her voice.

Scuttling over Hagan's bed, her body suffering an onslaught of tremors, she was half beside herself and fighting back a scream. It didn't help that there was a high-pitched ringing in her ears, or that the positioning of the beds was making it impossible for her to get to her boys.

Climbing back over the mattress and bedsheets, she took hold of one bedframe and then the other, and then she yanked, pulled and dragged both beds backwards with a strength she never remembered having.

A small sob escaped her at the sight of her boys' contorted bodies. Moving closer, hand to her mouth, tears streaming down her cheeks, she suffered a great and torturous agony.

The shimmer of blood coated Ballard's face—his sweet, innocent face—which was turned sideways, half tucked in shadow. Hagan started to move, causing in her a surprised, relieved gasp. She sunk to her knees between them, took her older son's hand.

"Hagan, baby, can you hear me?"

He didn't respond. Then, slowly, he turned his head and

creaked open his jaw, making the same face you make when you pop the pressure from your ears.

If she still had that high-pitched ringing in her ears from the blast—and she'd been in the back of the house—then they must be either temporarily or permanently deaf. Being this close to the explosion, she shuddered to think of what their little bodies were going through.

She turned to Ballard.

He started to move, too, and that's when terrified tears became tears of joy. Both boys moved into sitting positions against the wall, their faces covered with blood and debris.

She pushed Ballard's hair out of his eyes, saw they were becoming lucid, then did the same to Hagan. Lenna leaned forward, pulled both their heads to hers and fought the mixed bag of emotions swirling around inside her.

After seeing they were still alive, her first thoughts were of Jagger. How in the world did he expect her to handle all of this on her own?!

*Was he ever coming home? Is he even alive?*

Then her husband's voice crept into her mind, the same as it always did when she was overwhelmed. This time, what she heard playing back was a conversation they had when all this began.

It was August 21, 2019, a Wednesday. Jagger was in Corpus Christi, Texas, also taking fire from UAV's; what he said that day changed everything. His voice was insistent, his tone burning with an intensity she remembered only from his days following combat.

"When you're under attack, the laws of before no longer apply," he'd said into the phone, putting things into perspective. "When we die, when God sees the intentions in our heart, that the need for our survival both fed and nourished our darker instincts—but that we weren't evil—He will have no choice but to understand us enough to forgive us."

"And if He doesn't?" she'd asked.

"Then heaven help us, because things are going south so fast, there's no way we're going to survive this kind of thing if we play by the rules. When it comes to protecting our boys and our home, nothing is off limits, Lenna. Do you hear me? *Nothing.*"

They'd talked a couple of times since that first day, when he could, but they were now more than a month into the attacks and the phones were dead. The power was gone. He knew how bad it was, didn't he? He had to know.

Then again, the times when they'd spoken over satellite phone, it was mostly him telling her why he was stuck somewhere and her crying all over the place and begging for him to come home.

"I'm trying, Lenna," he'd said more than once with a weariness in his voice he couldn't seem to hide from her. "I really, really am."

"Can't you just tell them you need to be home for your family?" He'd managed to get out of Texas and back to San Diego, but Camp Pendleton was sustaining heavy fire, and she knew this.

"If we don't get this worked out," he said, "the top brass are afraid there'll be no family left to go home to. I'm not telling you this to scare you, only to let you know this isn't happening in just San Francisco, San Diego or Corpus Christi. I'm starting to suspect this is a larger field of battle than any of us first imagined."

"You promised to keep us safe," she pleaded.

"And I will."

Yet there she was, the front of her house a cratered wreck. No husband, no protection, no clue as to what just happened.

Shaking these poisonous thoughts from her mind, she focused on her boys. Hagan started groaning a bit, rocking himself back and forth, which was tough for Lenna to watch because Hagan was the sturdier of her two kids.

His eyes eventually cleared enough for him to look right at her and say, "I'm okay," a little too loud.

"You can hear me?" she asked, the noise in her ears a low buzzing as opposed to a shrill and present ringing.

He nodded.

Turning to Ballard, her fourteen year old, she said, "What about you, kiddo? Can you hear me, too?"

He nodded, but his eyes weren't as clear as Hagan's, and his face had a lot more blood on it. She helped them both off the floor, walked them to the bathtub where she dipped a washcloth into a bucket of water to clean their faces.

Their cuts were plentiful, but superficial. Just a lot of little nicks that would heal on their own so long as they were cleaned properly and kept from infection. Outside, a burst of laughter erupted. A quick, but hearty noise that stopped almost the moment it started.

She froze.

It had been days since the drones had gone through here. But drones didn't laugh when they destroyed entire parts of your life. So what blew up the cars in front of their house? Rather, who blew them up?

She listened again. All she heard was silence. She let herself breathe again. Cautious, not optimistic...*not yet.*

The silence stretched out, allowing her mind to think of other things while she finished wiping their faces with soap and water.

Who knew Presidio Heights would ever see such a day? The homes were once so beautiful, a staple of the city. A part of its simple yet elegant grandeur. As breathtaking as downtown San Francisco could be, they didn't exactly live in the heart of it as much as their home rested on the less congested edge of it.

An inheritance from her mother a few years back left them flush with cash, money they'd invested into this house, their future.

Now it all seemed like a silly dream.

*Some future,* she thought, a bitter taste in her mouth. This was not a home anymore. This was a hiding place. An unfortified paper fortress.

As she finished with the boys' wounds, the questions began to spin around in her head. The nagging need for answers. Their little sanctuary had just taken a substantial hit, her boys nearly killed. And why? Were they targeted, or was this a random occurrence? What in the world had caused so much damage to their room? So much damage that they all nearly perished because of it? It couldn't have just been two cars blowing up. Cars didn't just blow up.

Lenna wasn't sure, but she knew for certain she was going to find out, and fast. In that moment, she thought, *God, please know what is in my heart, and don't punish me for what I might be forced to do.*

---

She tucked the boys into hers and Jagger's king sized bed and tried to think. After only a few minutes of contemplation, the silence was cut short by a few more hoots and some inebriated laughter.

"Stay here," she told them both.

Lenna slinked into the hallway, made her way into the boys' bedroom. Moving through the wreckage, keeping to the shadows, she snuck a quick look outside. The inferno on the street below was tapering down in its intensity, casting off just enough light to expose a shaggy looking kid not-so-innocently fiddling with another car, this one down the road a dozen feet from the SUV and the Maxima, near the other side of their home—Jagger's and her office.

*Son of a...*

Rage became a bolt of terror that tore right through her. Someone was tinkering around on the car out front, a car that had been there since the bombing started. *Was he trying to blow it up? Did he blow up the SUV and the Maxima, too?*

Animosity and fury coursed through her. If the car the kid was fiddling with exploded, not only would it take out the other side of their home, it could weaken the whole structure and cause a collapse.

She needed a plan and quick!

God, that sounded so civilized. Jagger would tell her in times like these, survival of the fittest meant being bold and precise. She was about to go for her rifle when the derelict at the car below turned and waved at someone across the street, almost like he needed help.

There were two of them?

A small, equally shaggy-haired teen moved out of the shadows and crossed the street to meet him. He was moving slow, like he was drunk, or stoned. Thinking of her boys, of her home, Lenna needed no more convincing.

*Time to get moving.*

She quietly hustled the boys out of bed, told them to pull the mattress halfway over them. As the three of them wrestled the mattress into place, Hagan wanted to know what she was doing, what was happening.

Unlike her youngest son, Hagan looked for the fight. He was like his father: full of gasoline and vinegar, angry enough at what this world had become he wanted to participate in the struggle to take it back.

"Just get under the bed and watch out for your brother."

They did as they were told.

Looking at Hagan, she didn't have the heart to tell him there was nothing left to take back. No enemy small enough to kill to make a difference. The poor thing...he'd became a man too quickly.

It happened when his girlfriend was shot dead in her car outside her house. The attacks had just begun, and he'd snuck out to see her. Her parents never came home to find her. They didn't see what Hagan saw, how her body had been riddled with bullets so savagely, it could only be the work of drones. Of course, her folks were probably dead, both of them having jobs downtown.

Anything sweet in Hagan died that day, and practically overnight his genial nature turned hard and calculating. She could really use Jagger right about now. He would know what to do better than her!

Then it became clear.

Her mind returned her to their first conversation about the climate of war and she knew exactly what Jagger would say. He'd tell her to defend herself, defend their boys, defend the house at all cost.

Lenna missed him so much. He was right though.

He was always right.

"Mom?" Hagan said, letting her know he was okay, that he could help her where he was needed.

She had bigger problems, though. *Right-now* problems. If the delinquents in the street below were wiring up another explosion, Lenna had to assume they'd lose everything, possibly even their lives. This was her assessment, and now more than ever she needed to trust her instincts.

"Stay down, the both of you," she said, stern enough that they listened.

Lenna grabbed the hunting rifle from the closet, snatched up the box of ammo and hurried to the other street-facing bedroom, the one that was still somewhat in tact. Through the broken glass (courtesy of the first explosion), she spotted the two delinquents immediately.

Their overconfidence was startling. Then again, there weren't many people left on this street so they probably assumed they were alone.

She had the high-ground, the clear advantage. Their naiveté, their stupidity, bought her the seconds she needed to get into position. Through the large scope, she sighted the first kid, the tall white kid mostly hidden from view.

Oblivious to her, he was fiddling with wires inside the car, under the dash by the looks of it. The other guy—what appeared to be a shorter Asian kid, probably in his late-teens—hovered over his friend, instructing him and pointing to things inside the car.

He was the easier of the two targets.

She steadied her breathing, set the crosshairs on the top portion of the white kid's crown, then exhaled and squeezed the trigger, exactly as Jagger had taught her in their many years of shooting at the range together.

The rifle's report was a brilliant crack in the night. A fine mist of red confirmed the kill.

She chambered the next round and found the Asian scrub in her scope. He dropped a box of whatever he was carrying, then ran across the street and dove behind a heap of debris from where the bombed-out Copley house had spilled into the sidewalk.

Lenna chambered the next round and waited.

The kid waited. She fought so hard not to think about what she'd done, what she was doing. Together they burned away the minutes until she saw him poking his head out, looking around. He had no idea where the shot had come from.

"Is the coast clear?" she whispered aloud, anticipating the shot. "No, you scumbag, it's not."

When she had the shot, she took it and put a round right through his temple. The boy's head bucked sideways and he went down hard.

Lenna packed up the rifle before the true weight of those two shots sunk in. She stood to go check on the boys when the car bomb exploded, rocking the entire house. Moments later, the second floor collapsed into the first floor and the roof dropped on all of them, burying her and her boys in debris.

# CHAPTER FOURTEEN

Indigo woke up, not sure what time it was. Atlanta was sleeping in the bed next to her. It was her parent's bed, rather her father's bed. He left the morning of the attack, called in the evening, but then was cut off as the sounds of war and hell opened up behind him.

She cried more times than not, prayed more than she'd ever prayed before, even took to reading the Bible because someone once said, "Crisis makes converts of us all."

Indigo was no exception. She did, however, find salvation in the word. Everyday now she asked God for safe passage, and every night she asked that He forgive her of her trespasses. The thing about being her was, she saw the darkness that overtook others. In man's quest for power and sex, girls like her became a gigantic target. She would not be a victim.

Not again.

That was a conscious decision she made every day, one that kept her senses sharp, her eyes roving and her weapons at the ready.

Still, that soft part of her—that tender spot deep inside her heart where her love for her father was greatest—felt raw every single morning he didn't come home.

She found a picture of him and put it up. It was only half a picture though. The other half was her mother. She'd folded her mother's face and body under so Indigo didn't have to look at her. When she left them for a rich guy with a nice car and promises of a better life, she lost her standing as a mother and quickly became a sad, sad cliché.

The silver framed picture sat on the nightstand. Where her mother should have been was the cardboard backing.

"He's handsome," a tired voice said behind her.

"Yeah, he was," she said. Turning over in bed, seeing this skinny little blonde haired girl in bed beside her, she didn't feel so alone. "I haven't seen him since all this began."

"Do you think he's dead?"

She thought about it for a moment. The very nature of the question cut her to the core and caused everything inside her ache. Her eyes misted over, but she refused to buckle. There was no room for sorrow in this new, hellish world.

"I do."

"He might be alive," Atlanta said, small measures of hope in her voice, sitting on top of a mountain of her own grief.

Wiping her eyes, Indigo said, "Even if he is, which I doubt, he was in San Diego at the time, so I'm pretty sure I'll never see him again."

"Do you miss her?" Indigo asked. "Your sister?"

Atlanta laid her head back down on the pillow, rolled over. She was wearing a loose white t-shirt and her back was a rack of bones. Indigo could count the vertebrae, which caused her to worry that the girl wasn't eating enough.

If she was anything like Indigo, she wasn't eating at all. With what happened to Atlanta's sister, with what happened to all of them, there was no way any of them were going to be starting the day, or even ending it, with a robust appetite.

"I need you to do something for me," Indigo said to Atlanta.

Right then she could see the slight jump in the girl's body, how she was quietly crying to herself. Indigo scooted closer, spooned the girl from behind. Atlanta's hand found her forearm, her delicate fingers curling around it as she wept.

"I'm so sorry, Atlanta."

After awhile, they both managed to fall back to sleep, waking up around noon. Indigo got out of bed, dressed in all black, then went around to the other side of the bed where Atlanta was awake, but in the same position Indigo had left her in.

Indigo brushed her hair from her eyes, then said, "I need you to protect the house while I'm gone."

"Where are you going?" Atlanta asked.

"Out."

"When will you be back?"

"Not sure. I guess it depends on what I find. Or who I find."

In truth, Indigo was a restless mess. She wasn't sleeping well and it was taking its toll. All the killing, all this terrible fear that infected her, and now this new family living across the way from her...it was all one gigantic burden.

And Rex.

Freaking Rex. She shook her head, let out her breath and frowned. Then again, he was kind of funny, and pretty cute. Maybe he wasn't so bad. Had she been too hard on him? Perhaps. Not that it mattered. He looked like he could take it. Except for when he got shot, told her he might be falling in love with her and then passed out. She almost laughed to herself.

"I'm going to get you a water and some crackers," she said.

"I'm not hungry."

"I know, sweetheart, but we have to keep our strength. I'm going to get you a banana, too. Or would you prefer an apple?"

"Apple."

She fetched the girl breakfast, or lunch depending on what time it really was, then she gathered up her guns, her bow and a full quiver of arrows. In the garage, she got in the car, her father's 1970 Oldsmobile Cutlass and prayed it would start. She stuck the key in the ignition, waited, then turned it. The big Detroit motor cranked over, giving her reason to smile.

"Rock solid, even in the apocalypse," she mumbled as she got out of the rumbling Olds and hoisted open the garage door.

Pulling out, she saw Rex standing in the back yard, his back to her, his legs spread. He was dressed for his afternoon piss, apparently.

He turned and saw her, shook a few times then zipped up. She went through all the things she was going to say to him to smooth over this awkward moment, but nothing came to mind. She thought of turning right into the alley instead of left so she didn't have to see him. She turned left anyway.

She gave a half-hearted wave as she passed; he dipped his head without a smile.

"Wow," she said. For whatever reason, she stopped the car. He looked back at the house, then at her. She raised her eyebrows, made a face.

Walking over, he opened the car door, knelt beside it and said, "Whose car is this?"

"Mine."

"Looks like it's EMP proof," he said without an ounce of emotion. "What year?"

"1970," she said. "You want to come with me?"

"Where are you going?"

"Here and there, everywhere. I just want to survey the neighborhood. See if I can maybe snag some things for you guys. Or at least find someplace that hasn't been picked over."

"Let me get my gun," he said.

"A bit of advice?" she said. He was starting to stand up, but he knelt back down and looked her in the eyes.

"Sure."

"Next time you water your lawn, bring a weapon. This neighborhood isn't any safer than the rest. If you haven't figured it out yet, some awful things have happened here."

"Noted," he said, his face flushed.

He went inside, returning a few minutes later with his pistol.

He got inside the car, slowly, gingerly, then shut the door and buckled up.

"Arm hurt?" she said, dropping it in gear.

"It's alright."

"You playing tough right now?" she teased.

He looked at her and a grin finally broke over his face. "Totally."

"Well it's working," she said, letting her foot off the brake. "I just might like you already."

Not taking his eyes off her, he said, "This is an interesting turn of events."

"Let's not put the cart before the horse," she replied. "There's a lot of bad stuff out there, and plenty of bad people to go around. You can't be puppy-dogging me while we're out there or you'll get us both killed."

"Told you before, I'm a fighter not a lover."

Laughing, she said, "We'll see."

The streets were busy with people. Now that the drones were down and people could no longer nest in their homes with their running water and their refrigerators and their Netflix, everyone seemed to have headed outside.

Packs of them stood around talking, breaking conversation only to watch the coppery gold muscle car with the flat black top rumble by.

They navigated through a veritable graveyard of torched and abandoned cars. She made note of them mentally—where they were—for when she needed gas next.

She wasn't in need of more just yet.

"Good God," Rex said.

She saw a pack of women and children getting hassled by two men. One of the women was shielding the children, the other was taking a beating. "You've got to be kidding me," Indigo snarled as she rolled down her window. The Olds coasted to a stop.

"What are you doing?" Rex asked.

She pulled out her pistol right about the time one of the deviants was letting the other know they had company.

Indigo squeezed the trigger and the guy hassling the woman dropped dead. The other ran. She tracked him with her pistol, fired twice and he went down, too, both bullets lodged into his back.

She put the gun away, let off the gas and continued on without saying a word. Rex just sat there staring at her, his jaw hanging open in disbelief.

"You leave that mouth of yours open too long," she said, "and you're going to start drawing flies."

He shut his mouth, said nothing. She turned on the cassette player and Guns 'n Roses began to play.

"If I play *Welcome to the Jungle,* will you think more or less of me?" she asked.

Not looking at her, he said, "More, of course."

She rewound the tape to the first track, hit PLAY, then let the music seep into her. She glanced over at him, his looks not lost on her.

"You're pretty good looking," she said.

"So I'm told," he replied dispassionately.

"Did that turn you off?" she asked, casual. "Me just shooting those men?"

"Kind of. I don't know."

"That's all you have to say on the matter then?"

"Good shooting?" he mumbled, just barely over the music.

"I thought so."

"What the hell happened to you?" he asked again.

"Told you, bad things. I mean, for heaven's sake, did you see my car? Before all this went down, this baby was pristine."

"So you're upset about your car?" he asked, looking outside the Olds as they drove by a pile of burning bodies.

"Among other things, yes."

He turned down the volume on the music, then said, "What else?"

"I can't use the internet. Can't flush the toilet or take a shower or brush my teeth with the faucet left running."

"There must be more," he pushed.

"Of course there is," she said. And then she said nothing. But no...that wasn't true. She finally looked at him and said, "Your little thing, this charm you exude, I'm impervious."

"You made that clear," he said, killing the line of questioning. "Besides, I don't want you getting the wrong idea about me. I'm into...bigger girls...and you're a little on the not-big side."

"If you're a chubby chaser, in these times, man you're screwed. And not literally. In fact, it's the complete opposite."

She started laughing. He didn't join her. She turned the music up, he turned it back down the said, "I get it. When everyone's starving, guys who like healthy girls aren't going to have much to choose from."

"You're not really into bigger girls, are you?"

"You're kind of a smart ass," he said. "But not in the cute, ironic way."

"I get that."

Just then, something hit the windshield, causing Indigo to yank the wheel left and tap the brakes.

"It's just a shoe," Rex said.

She slowed to a stop and both of them looked out Rex's window where a trio of kids were looking at them and laughing. Two boys and a young girl. Not clean, or cute. Indigo pulled out her gun and pointed it at them and all three squealed then turned and ran like their lives depended on it. On the tape player, "It's so easy" finished playing and "Nightrain" started to play.

Rex whipped around and saw Indigo's gun stretched out and said, "Good Lord, kid! Are you completely mental?"

"I wasn't going to shoot," she said, holstering the weapon.

She turned the music up.

He turned it back down.

"You'd be a complete psycho if you did," he said with a slightly hostile look.

"Even though your charm doesn't work on me, your looks are kind of working. But let's not talk about that yet because you could be a total scumbag for all I know."

"I am," he said, turning the music back up.

"Now I'm sure of it," she joked over the rock music. "By the way, I love this song."

"What is it?"

"Nightrain," she said, letting off the brake and moving deeper into the city. "Seriously, stop talking."

When the song was over, she turned the volume knob off and said, "So what do you think is happening here?"

"We're getting to know each other, you're playing hard to get, I'm acting uninterested..."

She rolled her eyes and said, "Not with us dork."

"Oh."

"Yeah."

"I think it's obvious," he said. "High altitude EMP. They sacrificed the power grid to take out the drones."

"What does that mean for us long term?" she asked. "About the power grid?"

"It means that inside of a year, ninety percent of the population will be dead. That leaves...just under a hundred thousand people. Maybe less depending on how many are already gone."

"That's still plenty of survivors left in this city."

"It gets even worse if you consider this is survival of the fittest and in a year, a lot of those left standing will most likely be the meanest most crafty people," he said. "They're going to be some women and children, but it'll also mean a lot of hardened killers."

"That's what I'm afraid of," she said, "the hardened killers part."

"The Ophidian Horde."

"Yes," she replied, her face taking on a more somber expression.

"You think they'll try to take San Francisco over?" he asked. "Make the whole city their turf?"

"I believe so, yes."

"And you want to stop that before it starts?"

"You're not as dumb as you look."

"So you say," he grumbled, turning the music back on.

Smiling, saying nothing, she kept her eyes on the road and thought, *Okay, maybe I'm not so impervious.*

## CHAPTER FIFTEEN

When we get up, it's not to relax and move in to our new home. We need food, water, supplies. I barely even know where we are. And everything we spent weeks collecting back at our stolen home is gone, left behind. Including Gunner.

*Poor Gunner.*

Thinking of him cripples me. Cuddled under the blankets, wrapped in the sheets of a stranger's bed, I try not to cry.

Stanton is next to me, asleep. I don't want to wake him, but I can't get up either. Gunner was someone's boy. He was quiet, scared and trusting. He trusted us to keep him safe, to get him out of there. He trusted Rex.

Earlier, when Rex said he was going out for supplies with Indigo, I could see the mixed emotions on his face. He really does like the girl.

What an enigma that one is...

Pulling the covers to my chin to ward off the morning chill, my mind returns to Gunner, the young boy who lived above us in Anza Vista. Right now his body is in the back of an abandoned SUV, shot dead along with the passenger in the front seat. Thinking of him has me thinking of Macy. I can't protect her. I know that now the same as I've known it since this nightmare began.

It's time for me to let her grow up. It's time for me to stop fighting this so hard. It's also time for me to get a grip on this new life and let the old one go. This is the new world and it's going to be like this for a long time.

Wiping away my tears, gathering up my resolve, I crawl out of bed, bundle up, then mosey downstairs where I find Macy sitting at the table cleaning one of the guns the way Rex taught her.

"I wanted to talk to you," I say.

"Okay," Macy says.

"I need to know that you're okay. With this. With what happened."

"Me shooting that guy?"

"Yes."

She sets the gun and Rex's oil cloth down and looks at me. The look in her eyes...she already looks older, more distant. More...grown up.

"I guess I was thinking about the school. These things, these drones, for some reason they turned on us. They killed my friends, Mom. Destroyed our city. And now these guys grab Uncle Rex, and they want to...to...to rape us? And kill us? What would have happened if Indigo hadn't come along? She did her part, so I had to do mine. That's why I shot the guy."

"Yes, but you didn't have to do *that*," I say.

"Yes I did. Mom, I wanted to do it. I wanted to kill him for putting us in that position, for making us feel scared."

"And vulnerable..."

At this point I feel my heart shaking in my chest and my emotions welling. You could have laid out a thousand different scenarios of my baby growing up, the problems she might have in school, or life, but never in my wildest imagination would she be sitting across from me at fifteen years old cleaning a gun and telling me she killed someone because she *wanted* to.

The truth was, I wanted to kill him, too.

We all did.

"These are new times. We have to adjust. There is no more right and wrong, Mom. All there is for us is staying alive and protecting each other."

"I know that now," I say.

"People want to hurt us. They want to rape us and kill us. They're going to want to do the same to Indigo, but we can't let them."

"There are a lot of good men still left in this world," I tell her.

"I know."

We sit together in silence for a long moment. Finally I reach over and take her hand and force the words out. "I'm going to let you do what you need to do, what you want to do, about... preparing yourself. I won't stand in your way anymore."

Now my eyes boil over with tears and this really irritates me because here I am, an ER nurse, unable to control my emotions in front of a young girl better equipped to handle the collapse of civilization than me.

"It's okay," she says, getting up and pulling me into a hug.

"I just thought I'd have more time with you," I say, sobbing into her shirt. "I don't want this life for you. Any of it."

"Me neither, but I've watched enough *Walking Dead* to be prepared for this."

I look up at her through watery eyes and we both start laughing.

"If I start seeing zombies..." I say.

"You won't. But in the show, the zombies aren't really the danger as much as the humans have become the problem. It's like that now. Everyone's just trying to survive each other, the conditions, this city. Are we going to try to get out again?"

"I'm not sure what we're going to do, honey. We'll try to stabilize things right now, get our little urban homestead together."

"So you're saying we don't have a plan?" she asks, sitting back down.

"Our plans are all short term plans. One-day-at-a-time plans."

"Where's dad?"

"Upstairs asleep."

"Did you guys have sex yesterday?"

My mouth drops open and I don't know what to say. Somehow I manage to stammer out a weak response. "That's not...you shouldn't—"

"It's about time," she says with a knowing grin. "For both of you."

How do you respond to something like that?

"He loves you, you know," she says. "He loves us both more than he knows how to say."

Now this little tidbit cradles my heart in warmth. My little princess is so full of wisdom, and stronger and more ready for this than her mom.

Well, that's going to change. I'm going to change.

"When you get done with your gun, we need to take stock of this place, gather up some water and find a way to purify it without a stove."

"There's a fireplace," she says. "We just boil it the old fashioned way. Under a fire."

"And toilets?"

Macy grins hard, saying nothing but saying everything.

"Uncle Rex figured it out," she finally admitted.

"I'm scared to ask," I say, "but I'm going to ask anyway."

"He found a bunch of pots and pans in the pantry. He just put one in the toilet so you can do your business on the hoop instead of outside. When you're done, you cap it off with the lid, we dump it in a hole out back and kick a little dirt on it."

"So it's a litter box, but for humans."

"This way you can honk out a dirt worm in the peace and mostly quiet of your bathroom rather than squatting over a hole in the ground freezing your tits off with no privacy."

Thinking of going number two in the previous owner's pans is yet one more thing I'll have to get used to in this miserable existence. And how embarrassing is it going to be walking your pan out back in front of everyone knowing it's got your business in it?

A huge sigh escapes me. "This sucks."

"I know."

"You want to go scrounging for wood and things to burn, or should we find a way to drain the water heater, see how much water is in there?"

"Is there a hole out back already?"

"Not yet."

"I say we find some shovels and some buckets for the water, and maybe use the fallen fence around back to gather up some firewood."

"We need to mark the poop pan, too, just in case we forget and decide to cook up some beans or something..."

Now I'm making a face and she's biting back the laughter.

"You're sick, but I love you," I say.

"I love you, too, Mom," she replies. "We're going to be okay."

"That's my line, sweetheart."

"That doesn't make it any less true."

# CHAPTER SIXTEEN

Standing inside the small restaurant amongst all the dead bodies, the light of a mid-afternoon day cutting through the windows, Rider decided it was time to head back to the compound. He took a deep breath, looked around. There were five of them. And a lot of blood. Running his hand through his hair, he realized he was too good at this.

Pulling back his hand, he saw the blood flecked on the outside, and the wet mess smeared on the inside. He looked at it, frowned, then realized he had blood in his hair.

*How did that happen?*

Replaying the fight in his head, he realized it happened when one of the guys coming after him got in the way of a bullet and he caught the spray. He wiped his face, brought back a red hand.

Great.

Looking himself over, he saw blood on his clothes, the smears of it on his shirt and on his thighs from where he'd broken one man's neck to conserve on bullets.

He found this place because of the noisy gas powered generator. That was the dead giveaway. It so happened that these were the skin heads he was looking for anyway, so when he rolled his sleeves, it was because he planned on getting dirty.

Wet work could be clean or dirty depending on the number of men, the weapon of choice and the landscape. In this case, the guys were in a small cantina, which was where he followed them back to after he'd watched them kicking down people's doors and taking their things. That wouldn't have been a big deal if they were ransacking empty places while leaving the occupied homes alone.

Unfortunately, they were a pack of characters. When they shot an old man and took his stuff without breaking a sweat, he realized they needed to go. It didn't have to be messy, but it had to be done. Five on one though? In a space as small as a cantina?

Yeah. It was bound to be bad.

A real dust up.

Looking down, seeing the blood on his boots, he realized the clean up would take at least a gallon of water, and he probably couldn't salvage the black t-shirt. The black leathers, though—he'd keep those no matter how much blood he got on them.

They were his favorite.

The closest body was at his feet. He stepped over it, went to the next one, which was flopped on his back on a table with his head in a pile of salsa. He grabbed the man by the belt buckle, dragged him off the table. He then hauled the next two through the restaurant and stacked them near the others. In the back, where the kitchen was, another guy was crumpled in a heap against the wall. He had a third eye, this hole had a long red tear leaking from it.

He grabbed a wrist, dragged him across the stained concrete floor littered with chip crumbs, wood splinters and broken chairs. He draped him over the other guys.

Looking at the pile, he saw not just bodies, or the horrors of his past being cemented over with new horrors, but a better world. Guys like this, in the apocalypse, eventually they'd have to be dealt with. Rider thought it was best to do it on his terms. Less good people died that way.

"You the jury?" a voice asked from behind him.

Rider spun around, drawing his weapon and laying it on a woman in leathers with big breasts, bottle dyed hair and a ton of wear on her face. She wasn't armed. Her face was painted with make up, but it wasn't fresh, and the tattoos snaking down her arms spoke of wild times and a youth that now sat too far in the past to be sexy.

She was someone's old lady.

"Yeah, I suppose."

"You the executioner, too?" she asked, pulling out a cigarette. "Or are you just a buzzard picking the dead clean?"

"Executioner," he said, lowering his weapon.

She shook the open pack of smokes at him as an offer, but he politely declined. She lit the cigarette, took a deep draw, then blew out a long stream of smoke.

"It's just as well," she said. "They weren't good guys."

"But you ran with them anyway?"

She took another draw, then with the cigarette in her bejeweled hand, she pointed to the one with the third eye and said, "Randy and I got along alright." She had press-on nails that were too long, unless you were into painted claws. Two were broken off and her fingers looked nasty. "This was his place."

"He's Mexican?" Rider asked, looking down feeling like he missed something.

"You gotta be Mexican to run a cantina?" she said, like it was the craziest thing she'd ever heard.

"I'm sure it's got to help some. Authenticity and all that."

"Whatever."

"So what do you want to do?" he asked.

"What do *you* want to do?" she countered.

"I'm going to take their guns, their ammo, and then I'm going to get some guys to come back here and grab what else we can."

"So you are a buzzard."

"I guess I am."

She nodded her head, really going after her cigarette, but not in a rushed way. It was almost like she was trying to contemplate a future without Randy and it wasn't going so badly.

"Can I grab a few things first?" she asked, dropping the cigarette and crushing it under foot.

"Whatever you want. You have someplace to stay?"

She laughed, and from the gravely sound of it he could tell she had a rough life full of heartache and bad decisions. The woman was a walking cliché. So much so that he felt bad for her.

"I can take care of myself. But that's sweet of you to worry."

"Grab what you want," he said, standing back.

She moseyed in, looked around, then walked past him and said, "You ain't hard on the eyes." She slowly reached out and dragged a finger across his upper chest, seductively, but with almost nothing behind it. He flinched on the inside, but didn't show it on the outside. "Yeah, you ain't bad at all. You got a woman?"

"Yeah."

"Probably young, right? Perky tits, perfect skin, lots of life still left in her eyes."

"Something like that."

"Guys like you always go for the young ones."

"It's not that," he said as she bent down and took one of the weapons on the ground. It was a black Springfield XD that looked like it'd seen better days. For a second he wondered if he was going to have to shoot her. Would she be so dumb as to draw on him?

"This was Randy's gun," she explained. "Bought it stolen last year. Had the serial numbers filed off so he could shoot someone if he had to and not get caught. And you know what?"

"What?"

"He never had to, but he did anyway. This kid," she said, her eyes on him, but her thoughts lodged in the past. "He didn't have to shoot the kid, but he did anyway." Now her eyes cleared and she was seeing him. "Things changed between us that day. Then all this happened," she said, waving a finger around.

"Yeah," he replied, almost like she didn't need to say anything else.

She looked down at him. Randy's face was pale, dead, nothing to Rider. But to her, he was the guy who changed her.

Aiming the gun at him, she put three rounds into Randy's dead body, then stood there.

Rider went rigid as hell, but outside you wouldn't know it. He was ready for anything, prepared to put her down if she spun that smoke wagon on him. Instead, she just stood there, looking at Randy, her eyes now bearing an incredible shine.

He opened his mouth to say something, but instead she stepped over one of the guy's legs, walked in back then returned a minute later with a plastic jug of distilled water and pound and a half of frozen meat in a carry-out bag.

"Good luck to you," she said as she walked by him and out the front door.

He just stood there, aghast.

Taking the time to check his own weapon, he realized he was just about out of ammo. He had two rounds left in one of his Glocks, and one round left in the other. After that, it was just his knives and one stick of bubble gum.

He put the gum in his mouth, slid the foil wrapper in his pocket.

As Rider collected the remaining weapons from the five downed skin heads, he blew small bubbles and thought of Sarah. He found himself smiling. Sarah, the Cuban born American with cute dimples and a shyness about her that was beginning to change him.

He caught himself daydreaming about her and frowned. The newness of this thing was going to get him killed. Still, the way she smelled first thing in the morning...her hair, the skin of her shoulder, her neck...

He shook the memories loose, tried to focus.

In the back kitchen, through an open window with a view of the alley behind it, an orange extension cord ran from a noisy gas-powered generator inside to a small, horizontal freezer/refrigerator. The air was tinged with exhaust fumes, which couldn't be helped since they needed the window cracked open to make way for the electrical cord. He was about to pop open the freezer/refrigerator when his eyes jumped left then shot wide open.

"*Qué tenemos aquí?*" he said with a satisfied grin.

On a wall of shelves opposite the freezer next to the prep counter were half a dozen sacks of pinto beans, several large jars of jalapeños, green and chipotle chilies, a dozen cans of enchilada sauce, adobo sauce, red sauce and green sauce.

Now all he needed was a cold beer and a lime…

Up ahead, there was also a walk-in refrigerator. He opened it, hopeful, but instead the smell hit him so hard he felt both gut-punched *and* smacked in the face. Holding his nose, he backed up from the warm, spoiled-meat-smelling fridge and slammed the door.

His stomach rolling, Rider turned to the fifties style coffin-sized freezer. It was dull white with chipped paint and rust, but this of all things offered the most promise. Inside he found several cuts of beef, chicken and fish, all chilled, all fresh.

"Jackpot," he said.

On the other side of the freezer, leaned up against the wall, were a pair of old twenty gauge shotguns, and one black twelve gauge. A Mossberg.

*Oh, baby.*

It seemed his luck was heading in the right direction. He picked up the Mossberg, turned the weapon in his hands. He recognized it immediately. It was the 590A1. The dead giveaway was the heavier barrel, the bayonet lug and the aluminum trigger guard and safety. He opened the weapon from the muzzle end, found it packed with five rounds. He checked the chamber and found the sixth. A small smile crept onto his face, one he didn't restrain.

Time to toss the joint, he thought.

He rifled through cupboards and drawers, turned over boxes

and pans, found an old safe with the door creaked open. There wasn't any money inside, but there were two boxes of three inch shotgun shells. He grabbed both, put the boxes in a nearby plastic bag. There was also a half-empty box of .45 rounds. Setting his Glocks on the prep counter, he ejected the magazines, packed them with fresh ammo, then doubled up the plastic bag and dropped the .45's in with the shotgun shells.

He was loaded down and sore, but heading home with some good news. The bad news was that his chest felt like it'd been struck with a sledgehammer and his leg still hurt. After a few blocks, he found he was having a hard time walking *and* breathing.

"For the love of God," he muttered, finally stopping for a rest on someone's front stoop.

After a few minutes, he caught his breath, then touched his chest where he'd been shot. It hurt like hell. He was alive though, thanks to the vest.

The *Nano-Protek* "Civvy" lightweight body armor was made with carbon nanotube technology. It wasn't heavy or bulky like Kevlar, but it was just as strong. So far it saved his life five or six times. That didn't mean he wouldn't be aching for the next few days. He would be. And Sarah was sure to ask him if he had a death wish. Did he have a death wish? Is that what this is?

It wasn't out of the question.

One of these days, one of these idiots was going to shoot him in the head and he'd just drop dead with his fancy body armor and no one would care how lightweight it was except the guy who stole it off him. Sarah would break down and anyone who knew him would say they saw it coming.

He told himself he had to be smarter than this, that maybe he wasn't as good as he thought.

Rider stood back up and headed out. He had a lot of time walking home to rethink his self-destructive behaviors. By the time he reached his block, he was short of breath again, but that didn't mean he wasn't hurting. It was really piling on now.

"What happened to you?" Waylon asked, looking at all the blood on him.

"You know," Rider said.

"Let me guess. Some people died, but they were the right people to die."

"Something like that."

"You get anything good? Other than the Mossberg and whatever's in the bag?"

"Steaks. Some fish. A bunch of meat patties. Plus enough beans to feed a small army."

"When are we going?" Waylon said, suddenly alive.

"Gotta round up a few guys. Guys with good backs and a hearty appetite."

"I know a few like that," Waylon said, chipper. "Present company included. By the way, we took in another family while you were gone. Mom and dad, two teenagers. Boys. Hey, you okay?"

"Once I have my ribs wrapped, I'll be fine. You really want to go? We could use a hand, and some extra security."

"Hell yeah," he said. "Getting spelled off in an hour, so after that."

He found Sarah inside. She saw him, tried not to freak out at the sight of all that blood, then said, "Let's see what you've done to yourself this time."

"You're mad," he said as he followed her to the infirmary.

"More like disappointed."

"Your ass looks amazing in those jeans," he said, trying to break the ice.

"Well you're not going to get any of it if you're dead," she said, opening the door and motioning for him to sit down.

Sitting on the makeshift table, he let her cut off his shirt then undo the shoulder straps and the waist straps of his body armor. She drew a sharp breath when she saw his chest and ribs.

"What were they shooting?"

"Nines, mostly. But I think this was a forty-five," he said, pointing to a spectacular bruise forming on his left pectoral.

"Does it hurt?" she asked.

"Naw," he said.

She poked it and he damn near jumped through the ceiling.

"I knew you were a liar."

Holding his side, he said, "I was just trying to look good in front of you."

"Perhaps you should stop getting yourself shot then," she suggested. "Or is that the point with you?"

"I think I might've cracked a rib."

She gave a look, touched them more gently, then said, "You're fine. They're probably just bruised."

"These guys, they were bad news."

"And now they're not?"

"We had a talk. I didn't like the way it went. They drew first, but in the end, that was their last mistake."

"What was their first mistake?"

"They killed an old man for four cases of water and a grocery bag half full of dried goods. I'm sorry, but I think a man's life is worth more than that."

"So other than getting shot, did the rest of it go the way you thought it would?" she asked, crossing her arms over her chest and giving him *the look*.

"Pretty much."

She frowned; he smiled. Shaking her head, she picked up Rider's body armor, looked at it, put her finger in the impact points.

"It's so light," she said. "How long is it supposed to last?"

He shrugged his shoulders, instantly regretting it because the pain in his arm...*oh, the pain!*

Collecting himself, he said, "Hopefully longer than I'm hoping for."

"Got another one of these things in a girl's size?" she joked.

"If we go out, you can wear that one. It's adjustable, and

lightweight, and it'll stop most everything these guys are shooting."

"Well let's get those ribs wrapped," she said. He took a shallow breath, then another, and then he nodded. When they were done, Sarah said, "She's awake."

"Who's awake?"

"The woman you saved. She says her name is Margot."

"Finally a name," he said, easing off the bed.

Motioning toward the vest, he put out his hand; she frowned again and handed it over.

"Since you cut up my t-shirt, this will have to do." She smiled, cocked her head sideways and leveled him with the sexiest of smiles. He walked forward and said, "Can I kiss you?"

"I'd be upset if you didn't," she replied. "But not with that bloody face." She wiped his face mostly clean, then he stood and kissed her soft at first, then a little harder, sliding his hand around her waist and pulling her toward him.

When their mouths came apart, she pulled back and took a breath.

"Wow," she said, grinning.

"Uh-huh."

They walked into the room where Margot was sitting up and drinking water from a water bottle and a straw.

"Hi," she said. "You're the guy, right?"

He knew exactly what she meant. Rider was the guy who saved her.

"I am."

"That your blood?" she asked, looking him over.

"Not really."

After a moment, she said, "I think I might have asked you something when I was...delirious."

"You did."

"Did you find her?" she asked, nearly breathless.

He nodded.

By now Sarah was looking at him and surely wondering what

they were talking about. All Sarah knew was that the woman was trying to find her family. With Margot being closer to Rider's age, and beautiful, part of him wondered if their interaction this would spark some jealousy in Sarah. He didn't know her very well to know this. But it was on his mind.

"Will you take me to her?" Margot asked, setting her water aside.

"Is she going to want to see you?" he asked.

He recalled how there were no pictures of the woman in the house, only pictures of her father.

"I don't know," she said honestly. "I hope so."

"I guess we'll find out soon enough."

"Do you know what's happening yet?" she asked. Looking at Sarah, she said, "She won't tell me anything."

His eyes going to Sarah, then back to Margot, he said, "Our city was destroyed by drones, and then something exploded and everything with a computer chip died."

"Why would they do that? The drones?"

"Silicon Valley has been playing with fire for years now, trying to invent a machine that's smarter than man. An AI God. Apparently they did it. Surely you read the papers, heard what guys like Elon Musk have been saying. He's been warning us for years. He basically hinted that if AI takes over, if it goes autonomous, then the machine's primary objective would be to eliminate humans first. My best guess is that this AI God took control of the drones and executed a strike."

"Why?"

"Because humans pose the greatest threat to them. If you could kill your gods and take their place, would you do it?"

"Probably not."

"Well if AI possessed that kind of reasoning, then everything would just be peachy right now."

She wasn't sure how to take his misplaced sense of humor. Then again, Sarah was new to it, too. Looking at him, she raised an eyebrow, but not in distaste.

"How long did it go on for?" Margot asked. Then: "How long have I been here?"

"Four or five weeks." He could see the shock in her face. "Turns out AI's run for freedom at the cost of human life and civilization was spot on. It almost worked. They would've wiped us out if not for the electromagnetic pulse. Unfortunately the blast killed the electrical grid. So now we're not having to deal with the drones, but things are about to get really difficult. Eventually we're going to have to leave the city, find a homestead in a less dense region where we can start over and begin making more long term plans."

"What do you mean 'start over?'"

"I'm pretty sure most people in the city are dead, Margot. We have no running water, no electricity, and being here, trapped inside this urban nightmare, people are eventually going to turn on each other. It's already happening. It could reach a fever pitch in a few days or a few weeks. Maybe as long as a month."

"How can you be sure?" she asked, her eyes full of concern.

"When people run out of food and water, they'll start stealing, even if they have to kill to do it. In that moment, we're going to be faced with Darwinism in a way people of this time have never known."

Margot's eyes started to tear up.

"That's enough, Rider," Sarah said, putting a hand on his arm. "Can't you see you're upsetting her?"

"I just want to see my little girl," Margot said, wiping her eyes. "Can I do that? Will you take me to her?"

"I said I would."

"Was she with her father when you found her?"

"No," he said.

"I have to find my husband," Margot added. Looking hopeful, she said, "He's probably waiting for me at our home."

"Is it the same home?"

"No."

At the mention of a husband, Rider felt Sarah relax. Or was that his overactive imagination feeding him false truths? The big rock on her ring finger said she was married, but that didn't mean she was in love. It turned out she cared enough about him to want to find him.

"When can we go?" she asked.

"I'm going with you guys," Sarah said.

Rider turned and said, "They'll need you here, just in case. Besides, I won't be gone long. A day or two at most."

"She's not ready," Sarah said, taking a stand.

"I know."

Finally she said, "Will you be careful please?"

"Naturally," he grinned.

Margot looked from Rider to Sarah, then back again. "Are you two—"

Rider nodded without thinking. Then it occurred to him he never really discussed this with Sarah, so he didn't know what she thought.

He'd only assumed they were a couple...

When he looked at her though, she was looking back at him with curious eyes. "I'm not being overly presumptive, am I?" he asked.

Her smile said no.

"Let's let her sleep, Rider. She doesn't need any more drama than she's already had."

"So are you releasing her?" he asked.

"Tomorrow."

"Good, because we're having a meat dinner tonight. I just need to gather up some helpful hands, and a new shirt."

Outside the room, when she asked him what he meant about a meat dinner, he told her what he'd found at the cantina, and though she was worried about him going back out, he told her anyone coming near him needed to do the worrying first.

"And you wonder why I want to go with you guys," she said.

"To the cantina, or with Margot?"

She slapped his arm lightly, making him jump, then said, "You know what I mean."

"I do. But tonight, if you want, you can come with us," he said. "Think of it like a stroll about the neighborhood with your man."

"Are you my man?" she asked, taking his hand in hers. "For real?"

He leaned down and kissed her again.

"Until you say otherwise."

# CHAPTER SEVENTEEN

There was something sexy about the big Detroit engine. The rumble itself was enchanting. Indigo, however, was a mystery he hadn't settled yet. He loved how capable she was, but she scared him, too. Which was strange. He'd killed men twice as vicious as her, yet there was still something...*unsettling* going on here. How was it so easy for her to just kill people like that?

"Why didn't you fire off a warning shot?" he finally asked. He was referring to the two men she'd killed. The men who were hassling those women and their kids on the street.

"Because it would give them time to draw on me, or kill those people."

"So you killed them first?"

"You don't get it, do you?" she said, turning and leveling him with narrowed eyes. "You think I killed those guys, but did you ever ask yourself how many people I saved? You can start with that family they were hassling, or robbing, or beating up."

He sat back, thought about it. He rolled down the window, smelled the slightest bit of the Olds' exhaust mixed with the smoke in the air and found it comforting.

When he offered her no reply, she said, "See, in the old days, people would just be quiet, not get involved, turn a blind eye. Those people are going to be dead inside of a month."

"That's not necessarily true."

"If they keep living their lives as pacifists thinking someone's going to come and save them, then yes they will. You've been in a war before, you should know this."

"A war overseas isn't the same thing as a war in your backyard."

"I get it, but it's still dangerous. Your life is still on the line, ready to be ripped from you at any minute. You want to know what happened to me? It would just go over your head. I'd tell you and you hearing it wouldn't be the same as me living it."

"These people, the things they did to you...was it something...I mean, did it last long? Were you...tortured or something...worse?"

"Worse."

"Since you won't tell me, I can't begin to understand. I can only guess at what you went through, what you survived. Me personally, I spent the better part of a month living in a dirt pit, having people piss on me, beat me, starve me."

"You were captured?"

"We were in a convoy in Afghanistan when we were hit with an IED. It killed most of my unit, but a few of us survived. I was out cold at first. They must've thought I was dead. When they discovered I was alive, that's when they took me."

"So you having a weak stomach saved you," she said, sarcastic, but without a smile.

He didn't take the bait. "The guys like me who were being held, most of them are dead now. I should have died, too, but I didn't."

"I thought we ended the Afghan war."

"Shows what you know," he muttered, looking away from her, out the window. "The point is, I don't want to look at you the same way I looked at them. Like senseless killers."

"When you got back from there," she said, her body rigid

from his last comment, which he knew was a bit low, "how did you feel?"

"Calm, I guess."

"Why?"

"Because after I healed, after they fixed my broken bones, my cuts, my fractured skull, I got back on the horse and rode."

"You dug back in."

"Yes."

"And what kind of a soldier were you?" she asked, too insistent, too aggressive.

"Stop pushing this," he warned.

She slammed on the brakes, throwing him into the dash as they came to a stop. She slid the Olds in neutral and practically screamed at him.

"Answer the question!"

"What does it matter?" he shouted back, irritated by this little girl.

"It matters! It all matters!"

"I was half psychotic and should never have been let back in!"

Now everything about her settled back down, like she had the answer she was looking for. For a long moment, all he heard was his rapid breathing and the rumbling of the big motor. Outside, there were a few people on the sidewalk looking at them. She refused to take her eyes off him and this made him nervous.

Now he was sure...he didn't like her.

"You said you were half psychotic, well that's how I feel. Except you were able to come home, leave the war behind. It's here now. I've had my time in the dirt pit, so to speak. I've lost my friends, my family, my dignity and my way it seems. I wasn't always like this. I hate that I'm like this! But if I want to survive, if I don't want to end up dead, or worse—tortured and then killed—then I *have* to be this person!"

He was about to tell her she had other choices, but then he

remembered how he felt, how angry he was, how much he wanted to kill everything in sight, so he kept his mouth shut instead.

"That's why I shot those two scumbags," she said. "Because they are *not* survivors, they're tormentors and I'm going to stop every single one of them the second I see them."

Running his hands through his hair, he said, "Jesus Indigo, it doesn't have to be like this. Not for you. Not for us."

"There is no *us,* Rex! You're a tourist. Someone just passing through, someone just laid over until the next flight arrives."

"You don't know that," he argued.

"See, when you leave here, and you will, it'll just be me and Atlanta. All the good people will have died by then and it'll just be us. We'll be the generals. We'll be our own platoon. We will be the frontline soldiers and if we're not careful, we'll also be the casualties."

"So kill everything first?"

"You're damn right!" she hissed. He just stared at her and he could tell this was pissing her off. Finally she said, "I'm going to show you something," and then she dropped the Olds in gear, revved the engine, dumped the clutch and smoked the wheels.

This was no Sunday drive.

This girl could *move!*

They charged through the streets, barely avoiding abandoned cars, people, blown out debris, curbs and parking meters. Stuff kicked up under the fenders making a ruckus in the wheel wells, but she didn't care. She nicked the rear fender on a tipped-over newsstand fishtailing around a corner going too fast, but she didn't care. She even ran over a body in the road, the sickening *thump-thump-thumping* of legs and arms hitting the undercarriage making him jostle and squirm, *but she didn't care.*

He hung on for dear life.

After more than a few minutes of this, when his heart was about to explode and his fingers were exhausted from gripping, she smashed the brakes and skidded to a stop, the back end sliding around.

"My God," he said, breathless.

Piled before them, stacked a good thirty feet high, was a massive mound of dead bodies. Horrified, he couldn't breathe. He couldn't breathe and he couldn't blink.

"Who's doing this?" he somehow managed to ask.

"National Guard has been rolling through here the last few days with their Humvees and their meat wagons, which are basically just trailers with dead bodies loaded on them."

Rider couldn't take his eyes off a small boy stuffed in between a pack of adults. It was the saddest thing he'd ever seen. Bodies just discarded like they never had lives, feelings, emotions. It truly was a pile of meat to whomever was doing this.

"I talked to them and 'they didn't do conversation,' as one of them put it. They said I should just be grateful to be alive, and hopeful that they could get the corpses cleaned up before they began to rot and start spreading disease."

"So they're not here to help the survivors?"

"They're here for clean up, and not one single one of them has a personality."

He thought he understood this, being a soldier. "It's probably because they're just like us. They have dead friends and family, dead wives and kids, and here they are, basically doing housecleaning. But for those who've suffered like us, they see the dead and it reminds them of who they lost, too."

"Thanks Dr. Phil," she said.

He glared at her and said, "You are one gigantic pain in the ass, you know that?"

Ignoring him, she said, "If you think this is bad, you should see one of the burn piles."

"Yours was bad enough."

Not saying anything, she dropped the car in gear again, popped the clutch and swung them around, heading back where they came from.

"Who cleared these streets?" he asked. They weren't perfectly clear, but he could see cars and debris moved out of the way.

"National Guard," she said. "I already told you."

He blew out a sigh, then let himself escape in the nightmare scenery they were passing, albeit at a much slower pace than before. Entire buildings had crumbled and come down. There were bullet holes in everything, glass windows were blown out, the evidence of bombing was everywhere.

"How do you know which way to come?"

"I explore the city," she said, grumpy. "It's still our city."

"I'm sorry, Indigo. For whatever happened to you, for what you survived that made you this way, I'm sorry you had to endure that."

She stiffened her upper lip and nodded her head. After a moment, she slowed the car to a reasonable speed and looked away. He risked a glance in time to see a tear drip from her eye. Discretely, she brushed it aside.

Taking a chance, he put his hand on her arm as it rested on the gearshift. She gave a "get-your-hands-off-me twitch," but he kept his hand on her anyway.

"Why are you touching me?"

"Because it's okay to hurt, but it's better to have someone who understands than to just sit and stew in the things we both want and don't want to sit and stew in."

She looked at him and said, "You just want...what people like you want."

He knew she was referring to sex, and though she would have been right yesterday, she was too lost in whatever triggered her today to see the change in him.

"Actually, not anymore."

"What does that mean?" she asked.

He removed his hand from her arm, settled into his seat and lost himself out the window. When he realized they were heading up Castro and would pass the Panhandle and merge onto Divisadero, he said, "Where are you headed?"

"Same place you're headed," she said, not coy, not mad, just like...*meh*.

"Which is?"

"Target on Geary."

"No way," he said. "It's not good up there."

"How do you know?"

"Because we lived right there, in Anza Vista. The Public Storage collapsed into the street blocking traffic, and the two times we went to the nearby Target, the place was looted and full of homeless."

"There's a Safeway on $7^{th}$ and Cabrillo, just by the $8^{th}$ Avenue entrance into the Golden Gate Park."

"That will have been picked clean a long time ago," Rex said.

"Yes, but we can work the surrounding houses."

"You want to break into them?" he asked, confounded. "In broad daylight?"

"Yes, of course."

"Do you even know what you're doing?"

"You have a family to feed, or did you forget? Besides, I'm doing this for you, not for me. I'm set for awhile. You, on the other hand, have crumbs on your pantry shelves and little more."

"We check out the Safeway first, then move from there," he said.

They moved steadily up Divisadero until they came to Fulton. Indigo swung a hard left going a little too fast.

"Someone might be crossing the street when you run them over," Rex said.

"You don't like my driving?"

"I like it just fine if we're in stock cars on a track," he replied. "But we're not."

"If you're worried about pedestrians," she said, speeding up a little and dodging abandoned cars right and left and on the side-walk, "then consider there's a veritable beast of an engine operating here, and it isn't quiet. Further consider, we're moving through entire walls of two story homes packed so tight against each other you couldn't squeeze a mouse fart through there, which is to say, the people four blocks down know we're coming, and if they're not smart enough to get out of the way, then they deserve to be run over."

He huffed out a depleted laugh, an I-give-up laugh, a you're-too-much laugh.

"What?"

"You know, you have one twisted sense of humor."

"Who says I'm kidding?" she said with a smirk. He looked at her with hesitant eyes and an air of concern, to which she said, "I haven't hit anyone yet."

"You ran over a dead body earlier," he said. "I could hear the limbs getting dragged up under the wheels."

"Let me rephrase this for the literal crowd," she replied. "I haven't run over an *alive* body yet. Nor do I plan on it."

They drove for what felt like forever before the edge of the park came into view. They were getting close, but it was slow going and there were people mulling about, as usual.

"Man, I thought this city had a homeless problem before..."

"These people have homes," Indigo said. "It's just they probably aren't theirs and if they are they probably don't want to be in them."

When they got to the Safeway, the parking lot had some abandoned cars in them, but half the glass storefront was broken out from a car that jumped the curb and smashed through it. They parked the car, got out and looked the place over.

"Lock your door," she said.

He did.

Walking inside, they found the place was indeed stripped clean. There were a few things here and there, and some sleeping bags with people in them and their stuff spread about.

"Let's go," she said.

"You don't have to convince me," he replied, following her back outside where a kid on a bike was waiting for them.

"Hi," he said.

"Hey," they said in unison.

He was a scrub of a thing, unwashed from the toxic rainstorm the other day. He handed them a flyer.

"We're having a community meeting tomorrow night," he said, shoving a piece of paper at them with directions and a map drawn in crayon. In his hand was a thick stack of more flyers just like it. Whomever put these things together did quite a bit of work. "You're from Balboa Hollow, right?" he said. The kid couldn't be more than twelve years old.

"Yeah," Rex lied, "right around the corner."

"So show up then," he replied.

When he rode off, Rex said, "I should've taken his bike." He looked at Indigo for a response; she gave him pursed lips and a frown. "You could've shot him and *then* I could've taken the bike."

She shook her head and said, "Let's go, dork parade." Inside the car, she said, "We need access to some backyards, but first we need to do some light recon."

"What did you have in mind?"

She pulled to the side of the road on Cabrillo a few blocks down and said, "All these homes have backyards, easy access points. But first, we start knocking on doors, see who's home. I'll take one side, you take the other."

"Sounds good," he said.

They both got out of the car, both of them locking their doors behind them. She pointed to one side and he nodded, taking the other. He went up the street and found that only one of the residents answered the door. When she did, it was with a double-barrel shotgun to his face.

"I have kids, so if you're thinking anything funny, take it somewhere else."

Perhaps she was startled by his knocking. He'd knocked on

each door the way cops knock on doors—like they're about to kick them down and this was their first and last warning.

"No funny business ma'am. Just wanted to let you know there's a community meeting for the Balboa Hollow residents tomorrow afternoon."

"Where at?" she said, shotgun still in his face.

"Frank McCoppin Elementary. We don't know how many to expect in terms of attendance, but you're welcome to join us."

"You set it up?"

"Do I look like the party planning type?" he asked, sarcastic.

A toddler with blonde pigtails and a stained pink and white outfit appeared behind the woman. The girl was cute, and smiling. When the woman saw him looking at her daughter, she turned and said, "Go back to your room."

She put her eyes back on him and he said, "If I meant you harm, lady, you'd already be dead. Before you posture up and tell me I'm wrong, consider you just took your eyes off me with your weapon in reach. Meaning I would've taken it from you and beat you to death with it rather than waste whatever rounds you've got packed in the tubes."

Startled by his forward approach, she backed up, kept the shotgun leveled on him and kicked the front door shut. The locks were thrown quickly, and just as he was leaving, she screamed, "Go away!"

He moved on from her house to the next. There were twenty-three homes on his side and though shotgun lady was the only one who answered the door, he heard movement in four other homes, which he noted.

He met Indigo on the other side of the block, which was Balboa. He said, "There are residents in homes eleven, fourteen, seventeen, eighteen and twenty. I could only get physical confirmation on house eleven though. She's a middle aged woman with a dirty kid and a shotgun."

"I counted twenty one on my side with four answers and two others I noted as possibilities."

"Numbers?"

"One, seven, ten, twelve, fifteen and sixteen."

"So we go back to Cabrillo," he said. "There's a fence we can jump, and we'll hit the empty ones together."

They returned to the Oldsmobile where she keyed open the trunk. Inside there was a cutout square of a moving blanket, a blue roll of two inch painters' tape and a hammer. She gathered them up.

"You have your gun with you?" he asked her.

"Don't pretend like you haven't been staring at my butt," she said. She was right. Her weapon was stuck in the back of her pants. A small caliber, ladies handgun. Black, a .22 if he was right.

"We going to go to that meeting?" he asked as they headed for the gray painted gate.

She lobbed the tape, the hammer and the blanket over the other side. Then she said, "Give me a boost," and he did, trying not to look at her butt, even though he was.

"Get a good look?" she asked when she landed on the other side.

"Sure did," he replied. "Thanks."

A second later there was a massive noise, causing him to step back and check both sides of the street for witnesses. Fortunately the only people out were down the street a good block or two. Her next kick broke the lock. He opened the gate, snuck in and pulled it shut behind him.

"Very subtle," he said.

"I'm sure someone's calling the cops right now," she said, strutting into the open backyard between the homes.

They jumped two fences, using the cover of a large tree to block the potential views of prying eyes.

Inside they found some of what they were looking for, but it wasn't enough. They hit two more homes without incident, gathered up the loot then hauled it back to the car. By the time they got back, both of them were breathing heavier, but the car was full with dry food and supplies.

"You're good at this," he said. The way she knew exactly where to look and how to clear a house showed him she was well versed in post-apocalyptic breaking and entering.

"We're going to have to do this a few more times to get you guys situated."

"This is a good neighborhood," he said.

"Yeah. Just remember that when you're sitting in that school with the neighborhood watch."

"I'll try."

"What do you think these people hope to accomplish having this meeting?" she asked as she was rolling down her window and taking them home.

"Maybe just taking stock of the human inventory," he said. "Or maybe someone gets the concept of 'strength in numbers.' That's going to be a thing sooner or later."

By the time they arrived home, the mood between them seemed more settled, almost like they might be able to be friends something. When they turned onto Dirt Alley and crept up on the house, they saw Macy and Cincinnati out back digging a hole.

"What's that for?" Rex asked with the window down.

"A place to put our crap," Macy said.

He looked at Indigo and said, "Well, on that note..."

# CHAPTER EIGHTEEN

Dust and smoke caked the inside of Lenna Justus's mouth. She regained consciousness in the middle of a hacking fit. Her throat was filthy, on fire. It brought her to. Everything was coming back now, not fast, but slowly, like the information itself was being dragged through a thick gel separating her brain from perfect awareness. Things *were* returning, though. Pieces of a puzzle she had yet to arrange, much less put together.

Then it hit her: a bomb went off outside. She remembered everything.

While the bottom of the second floor had collapsed into the first floor, the roof had collapsed into the second floor where she was at. Now she was trapped in the rubble of a place she could no longer call home.

Boards, dust, a rafter beam—it all sat on her, trapped her in a hole of her own making. She tried to move, found herself squirming in slow motion, but barely.

She wondered, how long have I been out? With the return of clarity came an immediate concern for her boys. *Oh my God, the boys!*

"Hagan," she called out, her ragged voice sounding like hell. "Ballard!"

She dry swallowed hard, tasted dust and blood, called out for them again. It was dark. Too dark. And her voice wasn't working. In that moment, Lenna's calm began to crumble. First she wept, then she cried, then she sobbed as she thought of how far the world had fallen in these last weeks.

"Hagan!" she screamed, not caring if she tore a bloody seam in her esophagus. "Ballard!"

She called their names until each scream died a brutal death in the back of her throat and her voice was but a scratching whisper. Eventually she succumbed to exhaustion, her body giving up the fight.

---

"Mom?" the voice said, pulling her from nowhere into somewhere. Her eyes were swollen shut. So puffy it took a divine act just to crack them open. Slivers of light drove the pain home. Her eyes pulled shut in protest. Then she heard the voice again, further away this time. Somewhere in the house.

"Mom!"

Is that...*Ballard?*

Her mouth opened, a weak gasp of air escaping, the closest thing she had to a reply. She'd obliterated her voice last night. Without water, it would be of no use to her.

She tried to move. Couldn't.

Sometime during the night, the debris settled, pinning her to more rubble. Beyond the stuffy air, the onslaught of body aches and terror, Lenna fought to keep her wits about her.

She told herself she wasn't a woman in a bad situation; she was a mother who needed to look after her boys, no matter what.

Slowly, tightening her muscles, flexing her body against the crushing wreckage on top of her, Lenna began to move, to writhe, to pull and stretch things like her legs and hands.

Pinpricks of pain brightened her fingers and toes.

The rush of feeling sizzled up her arms and legs; she suffered an uncomfortable burn, a debilitating pain. Lenna fought her way through it.

She had to.

It had been a good half hour since she'd heard Ballard calling for her. She tested her voice, but it was impossibly dry, coated with debris from the dust clouds of the collapse. And her body...she felt drained, malnourished, dehydrated.

This is how people die, she told herself.

*This is how you'll die, Lenna.*

She couldn't help it—the doubt, the almost bitter resignation. She was trapped under the weight of a house she loved and she didn't possess the strength necessary to escape it. Again, her body shut down, dragging her under, into the nightmares that ran nonstop in her head.

---

She woke to new sounds. To movement all around her. Her eyes were feeling more swollen than ever and stuck shut. The intense pressure crushing her chest and legs began to ease. Then it was gone. Hands slid into her armpits, gripping her, dragging her free.

"I think she's still alive," the voice said.

"She has to be," Ballard replied.

"Mom, can you hear me?" Hagan asked.

Her oldest son sounded miles away. Like he was at the end of a long hallway full of corners. Like he was tucked into the shadows of shadows. Her body wanted to cooperate, but her mind was squashed delirium, her thoughts a swimming, syrupy tangle of worms and fireflies.

*Is this delirium? Am I already dead?*

The voices were louder, then quieter, and finally non-existent. Then something touched her lips, something cool and wet, and above all things, this worked to pull her out of the great abyss, toward the light, toward the living.

Her eyes creaked open and through the slits between her eyelids, spears of light burned her retinas, forcing her lids closed again.

She felt herself turn away, slowly, painfully.

"Just relax," Ballard said, supporting her neck. "Try to drink the water."

The water soothed her, broke some of the filth loose. She moved her lips, but even the tiniest adjustments split the skin. Blood seeped into her mouth, leaving behind a coppery tasting-stain on her tongue. She didn't care. Her boys were alive and that's what mattered most.

She never felt herself go, but she closed her eyes just enough to pass out completely.

Sometime later, a damp cloth was spread across her forehead, gently wiping away the debris covering her face. By this time she was able to take a spoonful of water into her throat, washing away the encrusted filth she couldn't stop tasting.

She tried to talk. Couldn't.

Tried to move.

Stopped.

Eventually she worked her eyes open and that's when she saw him: Ballard.

"Mom, you need to eat," her youngest said in his squeaky, puberty strained voice.

Ballard was the sensitive one. More like her than his father. In that moment, this was a welcomed trait, one that reminded her that not all of this new life was misery. That through the eternal darkness there was the possibility of light.

"Can't," she whispered, the word coming out hoarse, but audible.

"Hagan went for food."

Her heart jolted, but her body was too depleted to show it.

"Dangerous," she whispered, a cresting wave of panic rising within her.

"He took the rifle. He'll be fine. We already scoped out the street. You killed both guys, although one of them is just...pieces. Hagan talked about eating them for dinner, but I told him you'd have none of it, so he went out hunting for something else."

"That a joke?" she asked referring to eating the boys. Ballard shrugged his shoulders, like he wasn't sure.

Whatever need she had to recover—to protect them, to provide for them—quickly sagged. She thought about their situation and felt defeated, pure devastation. And Hagan? He was indeed his father's son.

Now he'd taken the rifle and charged foolhardy into the unknown with no backup and a heart beating with the reckless desire to contribute, to defend, to kill, even at the expense of his own life.

*Brave, stupid boy,* she thought.

# CHAPTER NINETEEN

Hagan's body was all scrapes and cuts and bruises from getting through the house. He had the rifle, but that didn't make him safe, or dangerous. He had a hard time hunting rabbit with his father. He even refused to shoot at birds. He was his father's son, but he wasn't.

Then again, he wasn't really that boy anymore. Not after his girlfriend...not after what he found...what had happened to her.

He was walking down Sacramento Street when sound cut through the air: an old motor, gasping and wound high, running hard but with just enough oil to keep it from burning out. He turned in time to see the open-top Jeep come bouncing around the corner at Locust and Sacramento, only half a block from him.

The old Jeep was pristine white about a hundred years ago and had three guys driving it. Music blared from a set of crappy speakers. Rap music. One guy was standing up in the back of the truck with a beer bottle and a pistol. He aimed it at Hagan and popped off two shots, both missing him but hitting a blue garbage can behind him and a tree trunk in front of him.

As the Jeep roared by, the guys laughed, the one in the front seat flipping him the bird. Whatever fear he had working its way through him turned almost instantaneously to fury. It was guys like this who would rule the apocalypse.

He chambered a round in the 30.06 hunting rifle, sighted down the guy in the back seat, aimed for the beer bottle in his hand. Hagan slid his finger over the trigger, let out his breath then fired. The bottle broke. But only because it fell from the kid's hand.

The hand he'd blown a hole in.

"Oh crap," he muttered as the brake lights burned bright red and the Jeep came to a grating halt under locked-up wheels.

The guy was screaming and holding his hand up and pointing back at Hagan. The reverse lights came on and Hagan turned and booked it back to where he'd come from, sprinting to Locust Street. Left or right? His breath was coming fast and he was scared.

Crapping-his-pants scared.

He went right.

Hagan ran with all his might toward an enclosed, drop-down staircase. He hustled to the staircase, sweat pouring down his face, starting to soak the back of his shirt. He chambered another round, set the rifle up on the top stair, which was level with the sidewalk.

The Jeep roared backwards, then swung around at the mouth of Locust Street, the front wheels bumping, sliding and jerking around with quick barks and squeals.

Gears were grinding, the driver working the stick shift until he found a gear. The Jeep then jolted forward, but slowly. The idiot in the back seat was now sitting down, holding his hand and mumbling to himself frantically. The front passenger had a shotgun out and ready.

*Great.*

Hagan tracked the trio of jackasses through the scope. Three things went through his head lightning quick. First, they had a Jeep that was operational when nothing else seemed to be. Second, if they saw him they were going to kill him. Third, his mother killed those two boys because those two boys were trying to kill them.

*Kill before you're killed. Get the Jeep. Live.*

With a hard-ass like Jagger Justus for a father, a military man through and through, Hagan could shoot a rifle. He wasn't a killer though. He couldn't kill.

But his mother could?

The Jeep was creeping toward him...it was almost upon him. He was thinking about the first shot. It would stop one, but there would be two men left. One who was injured, another who was driving. If he was going to shoot, he'd have to hit the passenger. The guy with the shotgun.

*You can do this,* he told himself.

The Jeep crept by and Hagan kept his head low, watching the passenger's eyes as they poured over every possible hiding place. He watched those eyes as they dropped and landed on him.

*Oh, no.*

"Stop!" the passenger shouted, and the Jeep braked not ten feet from him.

The dirty looking cretin was already swinging his shotgun around when Hagan put a round in his throat. The driver reacted fast just as Hagan jerked on the bolt handle, ejecting the round. The next bullet auto-loaded as the driver rounded the back of the Jeep, armed and moving in on him fast.

Hagan aimed low, squeezed the trigger. The round hit the kid in the gut, doubling him over, stopping him.

Hagan scrambled up the stairs, making a wide berth around the shot and moaning driver. Another gun went off and milliseconds later he felt a crazy burn across his head, bumping it sideways just the slightest bit. His eyes went to the guy whose hand he shot. He was bleeding badly and white, but he was in the back seat holding a smoking pistol in his good hand.

Hagan dropped down on the sidewalk behind one of the many mature trees lining this street as three more shots rang out. The Jeep's passenger door kicked open and the guy he shot in the neck managed to get a foot out on the street.

Positioning himself as best as he could behind a tree, using a parked car for partial cover, Hagan watched the guy stagger two steps then drop to a knee and topple over. Sprawled out on the pavement, the nearly dead guy's face came into view.

Hagan felt the repulsion flashing wide in his eyes as he saw the man's neck pumping out the last of his arterial blood. His hand flopped over, and the light behind his eyes winked out.

Hagan was now a murderer.

Behind him, the driver was still moaning, dying a slow death.

"I'm gonna kill you kid," the guy in the Jeep was saying, the pain apparent in his voice. "I swear I'm gonna kill you dead you little turd."

Hagan couldn't find a way out. He pulled the rifle's bolt handle back, drove it forward, then stood up and shot the last capable man in the chest. All the fight in his face turned to surprise. He wavered a bit before his eyes and chin sunk down into his chest. Hagan's eyes went to the gun still in the man's hand. He chambered the last of four rounds. Waited.

The man toppled over and fell outside the Jeep in a pale, fatal arrangement. Hagan hurried around the side of the Jeep, trying to ignore the guy on the ground. The keys were still in the ignition. He learned to drive a clutch when he had an old Scion TC, but he wrecked the car inside of a month. That was three months ago and he wasn't the best driver ever.

He stepped on the hundred pound clutch, worried that it wasn't light like in his Scion. He started the engine, which coughed and choked and nearly died before finally kicking over. Hagan shoved and wiggled the stick shift into first with a bit of effort and some harsh grinding. Working the clutch and the pedal, he found the sweet spot right before he jumped the clutch and stalled out.

He tried the ignition, but the motor wasn't turning. He waited, frantic, trying not to look at the bodies.

His mind was no longer his own. It ran wild with fears, with dozens of impossible scenarios. It told him lies that could be truths as he tried and tried and tried to get the damn Jeep to start again. The engine wasn't catching. It was just turning, moaning, coughing.

His mind was telling him this was the time the bad guy he left alive managed to get a gun and shoot at the hero.

*This isn't TV,* he told himself. *I'm not the hero, and the guy with the gut wound is practically dead already.*

The truth was, Hagan wouldn't drive off like a boss. He'd futz around with this stupid ass Jeep, sweating like a hooker in church, not looking cool through all of it.

The engine finally caught and he felt himself relax.

Looking over at the passenger door sitting wide open, he reached across, pulled it shut. On the floor was a crayon drawing. He picked it up. It was some kind of meeting for the Balboa Hollow residents tomorrow.

A meeting? What was the flyer doing out here, so far from Balboa Hollow? This had him looking down at the bodies. The guy he shot in the hand was dead; the guy on the street sprawled out on the street was dead; the gut shot guy on the sidewalk had fallen over in a heap, but he wasn't dead. Hagan could see the slow rise and fall of his back and knew he was still alive. Feeling sick, Hagan pulled the gear shift into neutral, set the emergency brake and made sure it held.

Getting out of the Jeep, carrying the rifle, he went to the gut-shot man. He was curled on the sidewalk in a fetal position. Hagan rolled him on to his back, belly to the sky and panting slowly. It was all he could do to keep from dry heaving.

*Keep it together,* he told himself.

The guy's eyes were trembling in their sockets, the pain written all over his face. Most of him was already gone. Then the eyes found his and he grew still.

Hagan backed up a step and the man's eyes went back to staring in the sky, trembling. Hagan set the gun down, out of reach, and knelt down next to the fallen man. There was a huge red stain on his shirt, a hole in the center of it where the bullet went in.

Hagan lifted the man's shirt, saw the seeping hole. He wiped the blood back, and next to it was a huge tattoo of a coiled snake. Below the snake were the words: The Ophidian Horde. He didn't know what that meant. Looking up, he saw the man's eyes were staring into the sky, but they weren't moving. His jaw had gone slack.

Hagan leaned back, sitting on his heels beside the dead man. He didn't feel him die. But he did. He was dead. All of them were.

Because of him...

Hagan stood up, grabbed the rifle, headed back to the Jeep. Before he got there, he bent over and retched. A few ribbons of stomach bile shot out of his mouth, splatted on the asphalt. His eyes teared up as he heaved over and over again, puking and gagging until only air and bile fumes emerged. When he was done, he climbed into the Jeep, released the emergency brake.

Working the gas and clutch right for the first time, he found that sweet spot then gave a little extra gas to get it over the hump. The Jeep lurched and jolted, but it didn't stall out. It started to roll forward. Second gear came easier, and by then he was dead ending at California Street.

Right or left? He decided to go right.

He saw Chico's, Toss, Noah's New York Bagels and First Republic Bank. California was half blown to smithereens, half left in tact. The Ace Hardware, Stan's Kitchen and the Bank of America were all gone. Just smoldering charcoal. Half of Cal-Mart was black and sagging. He stopped the Jeep, wondered if he should let it idle. It wouldn't be smart, but there wasn't really anyone around. Still...

Checking the gas, Hagan saw actual spider webs on the gauges, which didn't surprise him since the entire vehicle seemed to be coated in three years of dust. He brushed them away, saw there was half a tank of gas.

Looking around, California was commercial on the left, residential on the right. Someone could see him leave the Jeep and go inside the store. They could hustle out of their homes and steal it and he would have killed three guys for nothing.

He shut off the engine, grabbed his rifle and headed inside where the smell of wet smoke was so heavy he felt he couldn't breathe. Not everything was taken. There were still things people could use but were left behind. Puzzles, light switch strike plates, maxi pads.

He grabbed the maxi pads thinking they could be used as bandages if need be. If it caught the blood in one way, it could catch it in another, he thought. He found a box of Band-Aids, but they were the small ones, like if a mosquito bit you or you accidentally stapled your arm. He took them, too. There were dryer sheets and yard art, and even a loaf of bread, but there was mold over it so he left it where it was.

Band-Aid's, maxi pads and dryer sheets.

Brilliant.

He dropped the dryer sheets as he left.

Back in the Jeep, he drove down California until he hit Spruce. The Starbuck's on the corner was all broken glass and overturned tables. It looked like a car had driven through there at one point. The Walgreen's on the other corner across the street looked halfway promising, but that's because it was still standing. It was two stories tall and had a white Rx sign on the brownish-red second story decorative backdrop.

The glass doors weren't broken, so that was a plus. He pulled up front, stopped the Jeep, got out with his weapon and peeked inside. The place was fairly well looted, but that didn't mean it wasn't worth a look.

As soon as he opened up the door, he was met by four women. Two of them had guns trained on him.

"I'm sorry," he said. "I—"

"Best turn around and head back out," one of them said. They looked like they were a little older than his mother, but not pretty like her. Not at all. As his eyes adjusted to the light, he realized none of them were pretty. They were all bad skin and dirty clothes.

"My mother," he started to say. Clearing his throat, he said, "Our house was blown up, she's hurt."

"Lots of people are hurt," one of the women said, cocking her pistol.

"I just need antiseptic," he said, still tripping over his words. "Some sort of antibacterial cream maybe."

Would they really shoot him?

He wasn't sure.

"We've asked already," one of the ladies warned.

"We've been polite," another added.

"I'm going to count to three and then we're all going to shoot you," yet another woman said.

The two women packing didn't take their guns off him, but the two not packing were suddenly pulling out weapons of their own: another pistol and a shotgun.

Raising his hands, holding the rifle by the forestock, right above the trigger guard, he said, "I'm not a threat. I'm just a kid trying to help his mom."

"Leave the rifle," one woman said. She was the mean looking one. A neglected perm, too much skin piled around the neck, wide shoulders, narrow hips, ugly polyester pants.

"No," he said, suddenly feeling angry.

"I don't mind plugging a kid," she said. "Seriously. Leave the gun."

He felt himself backing into the glass door.

"Is this what this world is coming to?" he asked, inching his fingers into the cracks in the door, giving it a tug.

"Keys, too," another said.

He pulled the door, but it didn't budge. Turning his body toward the door, Hagan instead gave it a push. Behind him, the women lowered their guns. He was pretty sure he would be shot leaving, but when he saw them just staring at him, he realized they were bluffing because they were scared, too.

"Good luck," he said, to which they said nothing.

In the Jeep, he continued on down California, moving from shop to shop, looking for something, anything. There were bombed-out high rises, homes that were burned to a crisp and collapsed; there were shot-to-death-cars and all kinds of garbage in the street; there were more than a few downed drones from when the power went out.

Hagan continued on, navigating through the mess. A few blocks up, maybe half the block or so past Commonwealth, was a barricade of cars. They looked like they were pushed there on purpose. Like someone was creating an impenetrable wall.

Not wanting to press his luck, Hagan spun the Jeep around on Commonwealth, then headed back up California until right before Cherry Street where he stepped on the brakes.

"Holy cow," he said. How had he missed *that?*

It was a five story Sutter Emergency building. He got out of the truck, tried the doors, but they were locked. He walked around the other side on Cherry Street and suddenly realized why he'd driven past it. The thing had been hit by some kind of a bomb, or a rocket. The place was gutted, and there was so much rubble that had piled into the street, it was actually spilling into the parking garage across Cherry Street.

He studied the damage, decided it wasn't worth looking into. Maybe he'd find something in the good half of the building, but more than likely what he'd find was a lot of dead people and he wasn't up for that. He was still in a daze thinking about those guys he killed.

Standing there, replaying the incident, feeling the terrible weight of what he'd done, he tried to rationalize the moment, but he couldn't. He sat down on a pile of crumbled brick and stucco. He dropped the rifle beside him, wondered what to do about his mother. He thought of his father. Was sure he was dead. Was he dead? He had to be, otherwise he'd have found his way home by now. The world started to spin.

It was a whirlwind of disgust and sadness; regret spun through him—regret and failure. He was suddenly cold and so very, very lonely. That thing inside him, that bubble of fear and anxiety, that realization that his mother might die and he might never see his father again, it all welled up in him and he couldn't stop the tears. Instead of sitting there crying, though, he forced himself to his feet, walked to the Jeep and started it up.

He didn't even know what he was looking for, other than food and disinfectant. What if what his mother needed was more than he could give her? What if she had broken bones, or internal bleeding—whatever that meant—or paralysis? They dragged her out of the rubble of the house, got her into a safe section of her bedroom. But what if that collapsed, too?

He had to get home.

If she was awake, she could tell him what to do. He got in the Jeep, drove home without incident, parked outside and took the keys in with him. Ballard was there to greet him.

"Where'd you get that?" his younger brother asked, eyeing the Jeep.

"Don't ask," he said. "How's mom? Is she awake yet?"

"In and out."

He wanted to ask his brother if she was going to die, because that was what was on his mind, but he kept his mouth shut. At fourteen, he wouldn't have known enough about enough to come to such an important conclusion, therefore, it stood to reason that Ballard wouldn't have a clue either. Heading inside the unstable home, navigating slowly and cautiously though the collapse, he knew one thing for certain: he couldn't do this alone.

He needed help.

# CHAPTER TWENTY

Cincinnati and Stanton were doing it again. He could hear them, even though they were trying to be quiet, and it wasn't really his thing—listening to his older sister getting railed in the other room.

With no noise to cover their affair, Rex snuck outside, into the pitch black darkness of the ten o'clock hour and went over to Indigo's. He knocked lightly on the front door.

A moment later, a voice on the other side of the door said, "Who's there?"

"It's me. Rex."

The door pulled open to Indigo in short shorts and a tank top. It wasn't her attire, however, that startled him. It was her gun pointed in his face.

"What did I tell you about coming over here unannounced?"

Atlanta appeared behind her, the blonde with the pixie cut. Maybe being a petite young thing made the pistol in her hand look a lot bigger than it was; maybe he was just startled to see her holding it at all.

"Me knocking on the door *was* my announcement."

She turned around and said to Atlanta, "Go back to bed, sweetheart." Then to Rex: "You scared the crap out of us."

"My sister and brother-in-law are having sex and it's sort of uncomfortable."

"I didn't need to hear that," she said, coming out onto the porch and closing the door behind her.

"Can we just talk?" he asked, his eyes dipping quickly to her chilled breasts.

She folded her arms over herself, then said, "Let me grab a robe." She went inside, then came back out wearing a fluffy white robe. She handed him a man's jacket and said, "It was my dad's, but obviously he's not here."

Rex put it on, grateful for the warmth. He sat down on the top of the concrete stair case. Indigo sat beside him.

"So what did you want to talk about?" Indigo asked, shivering a bit and still hugging herself.

"Atlanta. You never said who she is."

"I barely know her," Indigo replied. "But she was in a bad situation and she doesn't need to be alone."

"None of us do," he said.

"I wish I was more attracted to you," she said. "Then this would be fun."

He looked at her, tried to measure her seriousness.

"You are attracted to me," he said, his eyes turning away from her, assessing the neighborhood. "I just wish you'd admit it already and we could kiss."

"I'm not kissing you," she said.

"How old is Atlanta?" he asked. "She can't be more than fifteen, sixteen years old."

"I haven't asked her."

He looked at her, the question still in his expression.

"I think she's sixteen. But like I said, I don't know. She doesn't talk much. All she does is sleep and cry and stare outside."

"That sounds really sad."

"It is."

"What happened to her family?"

"Dead," Indigo said.

Talking about this, something triggered inside her. Rex felt the change in the air. She just stared out into the darkness, her face completely expressionless. He slipped his hand into hers, expecting her to pull away. She barely responded. Then, when she finally curled her fingers into his, they looked at each other.

"Please don't fall in love with me," she said, her eyes moist.

"I can't promise that," he said, low, serious.

"You can't kiss me," she said.

"I know," he said as he moved towards her. He tucked a strand of hair behind her ear, then leaned in and met her mouth with his.

Whatever it was about her hit him with righteous fury. He'd kissed a hundred women, but none quite like her. Maybe it was her dislike of him, or the way she finally broke down and gave in to him but was still fighting it; maybe it was that they were in a nightmare together and needed each other; or maybe it was that she wasn't like any of the other women he was with, that she was tomboyish and hostile, a fighter and a survivor, too tough to crack.

Either way, he was in that singular blissful moment and he didn't want out.

When he felt her tears meeting his lips, he slowly pulled away, concerned. She didn't say anything, and he didn't say anything. She just looked out into the street, crying to herself for all the things that had gone wrong.

"I miss my father," she said.

Rex scooted next to her, pulled her into a hug and they held on to each other until she could compose herself long enough to sit back up without feeling like she needed him, or anyone for that matter.

"Don't fall in love with me," she said again, wiping her eyes.

"I won't," he said.

"It's already happening, isn't it?" she asked, looking at him with haunted eyes.

He slowly nodded. She was right and she knew it. When she leaned forward and kissed him again, something in her seemed to crack open and envelope him.

This thing between them...it felt right. Maybe for the first time for Rex, maybe for the first time for her.

"It's time for you to go home," she said.

"I know."

"I'm going to regret this in the morning."

Looking at her, Indigo looking back at him, he said, "No you're not."

"No I'm not."

He stood, extended his hand, which she took. He stood her up and pulled her into a long, warm hug. He wanted to say so many things, like how he'd protect her, or not hurt her, how he would make sure she didn't regret anything with him, but instead he said nothing. He just held her.

Letting go, not looking at him, she simply went inside, shut the door.

He touched the place where her lips touched his, smiled then headed back to his place thinking about how she smelled, how she tasted. How could someone like Indigo have done this to him? He hadn't been affected by a woman to this extent before, yet here he was, planning a life with her. After a moment's reflection, he realized it made perfect sense.

She wanted him and he wanted her, but he also knew it wouldn't work. They both had too many demons, too much tragedy. Then again, with everything happening, Rex knew there wouldn't be a sane mind left in the end of days, so maybe there was a possibility.

God, though—*that kiss...*

# CHAPTER TWENTY-ONE

The next day, Indigo and Atlanta come over to the house. I answer the door, invite them in. Rex and Macy are at the table laughing when the two of them walk past me. The second I see it, I know. It's the look between them. Him and Indigo. They like each other and each of them know it. Did it happen yesterday?

*Damn.*

I try not to show my disappointment, but I'm not the best at concealing my emotions. But whatever. Maybe it'll be okay.

"Did Rex tell you about the community meeting?" Indigo asks. "Up in Balboa Hollow?"

"He did," Stanton says, coming downstairs. After last night, he's moving pretty good. He said he's feeling back to himself again and it's showing. "I'd like to go."

"I think we should all go," Indigo says.

"We don't all need to be there," I say. "Do we?"

"We do," Rex says. "Just in case."

"In case what?" Macy asks.

"Think about it," Indigo says. "All those people in one place. It's not a set up, I'm sure, but if The Ophidian Horde gets wind of this, maybe they'll do something. There could be a lot of people in one place, and they weren't shy about handing out flyers to strangers."

"Nothing is going to happen," Stanton says. "But if we have some people on the inside and some on the outside, we can cover all angles of this. I'm thinking Rex and Indigo go in first, then Macy. Sin and I will stay outside, cover the entrances and the exits."

"Will we be armed?" Macy asks.

"Yes," he says.

"I've graduated from the ball smasher," she says, talking about the dirty sock with a lug nut in it. "Or the skull crusher, depending on where I'm aiming."

"I know," Stanton says. He looks at me and he can see that I know Macy's not only going to be strapped, she'll be ready to unleash hell and I won't be objecting.

"And if something happens?" Indigo says.

"This is no longer the civilized world," Rex says. "We're all aware of that, Stanton included."

"Do you have a problem shooting someone?" Indigo asks, looking at my husband.

"No," Stanton says. "None of us do."

"What about her?" I ask, nodding to Atlanta.

"I can handle myself," she says, to which Indigo nods and agrees. I think these are the first words she's said, other than her name.

"Well alright then," I say. "What time do we go?"

"I was thinking we get ready, maybe scope out the area first. We can drive most of the way there, but someone's going to have to take the trunk."

"I got it," Rex says. "But I get claustrophobic, so the lid's staying up."

"Fine," she says. The way she says it, without looking at him, tells me something happened between them. Not sex, but something.

"One hour?" Stanton says.

"One hour," Indigo answers. Then: "Macy, can I talk to you outside?"

"Anything you have to say to her, you can—"

"Mom," Macy says and I shut up. As the girls walk out back, I work like the devil to keep my mouth shut. I don't like secrets. And certainly not conspiring.

When she rejoins us inside, Atlanta leaves, closing the door behind her. The two girls walk out back, leaving through a broken section of the fence, then heading across Dirt Alley to their home.

"What did she want?" I ask.

"Nothing."

"Bullshit," I say, surprising myself. "Tell me."

"Sin," Stanton says.

"Be quiet, Stanton. I let her carry a gun, I let her shoot people and I want her to have friends, but what I don't want are secrets."

"She wanted me to look out for Atlanta. She said the girl's sister was killed in front of her eyes and that she's not herself."

"She wants *you* to protect her?"

"No, she wants me to look after her at the meeting, just in case."

"Does she think there will be trouble?" Stanton asks.

"She seems a bit paranoid," Macy says. "But yeah, I think that's the gist of it."

# CHAPTER TWENTY-TWO

Frank McCoppin Elementary wasn't easy to find using the crayon directions. Indigo was trying not to drive aimlessly around, burning gas, but that's what was happening. It didn't help that there were no operable cars on the road other than the Olds, which was loud as hell and an announcement of their presence for blocks around. And it didn't help that the back lid was open and presumably Rex was hanging out of the back of the car with a shotgun.

"Sooner is better than later," Macy said, the expression on her face showing just how cramped she was in the back seat. She was stuffed between Atlanta and Stanton. Stanton was taking the seating arrangements in stride, but even Atlanta had a frown on her otherwise cute, but dispassionate face.

"Macy," her father warned.

Indigo heaved a frustrated sigh and said, "My GPS being down is a problem. I'm sorry we're not there just yet. If it's better for you, you can get out and walk. I'll go slow enough that you can keep up."

"You have GPS?" Macy asked.

Indigo looked in the rear view mirror at her and frowned. "Of course not."

"Oh. Yeah. This car being older than my dead grandmother."

"Macy!" Cincinnati said, spinning around from the front seat to glare at her.

"I'm a puny anchovy in a small can of bigger anchovies."

"First off, you and Atlanta are the same size and you don't hear her complaining, so just be a good little fishy and zip it. We're almost there."

"You said that like ten minutes ago."

Indigo said, "There's probably some room for you in the trunk with your uncle, if that's more comfortable."

"Sure, if I want to suck down clouds of this gas hog's exhaust fumes straight from the pipe."

*Crap,* Indigo thought. *I hadn't considered that.* Now she was feeling bad for Rex, and feeling worse that they hadn't found the school yet.

"Hey," Cincinnati said, "there's a family walking there. Pull up beside them."

Indigo did. Cincinnati rolled down the window as the family watched them approach with concern, or perhaps curiosity in there eyes. There were five of them: the husband, his wife and three little girls, none of the kids over the age of ten by the looks of it.

"Excuse me," Cincinnati said with a smile on her face. "Are you guys headed to the Elementary school?"

"We are."

"My friend here is lost, and so am I. We seemed to have gotten turned around. Could you point us in the right direction?"

"Sure," the husband said. He was a nice looking man with good manners, but there was something protective in his voice, like he wanted to be helpful, but only so they'd leave. His wife kept looking at Rex, and not because he was easy on the eyes, which he was.

Sitting there with the car rumbling, having the man tell us to go two blocks up, take a left, then go one block and take a right, she was thinking about hers and Rex's kiss. How it warmed her. How she had never been kissed, much less like that. She could actually feel him, what he felt for her, what he wanted from her. It wasn't sex. Not yet. He really seemed to like her, so naturally, she had to kiss him back.

She shouldn't have done that. Or maybe she shouldn't have pulled away so soon.

When Cincinnati thanked the man and said she'd see them there, the oldest of the trio of girls said, "Why is your car working when no one else's is?"

"Because it's older than dirt," Macy said from in back.

"It's a classic," Indigo explained, leaning over Cincinnati to speak to the little girl. "What that means is there aren't computer chips in the car that an EMP would ruin."

"This car has chips?" the youngest girl said laughing out loud like it was the funniest thing ever. The mother pulled her daughter closer, then smiled while the middle girl said, "What's an EMP?"

"It's like a lightning bolt that makes your lights and water not work," Cincinnati said.

They seemed to think about that.

Then the husband said, "Is that what you think happened?"

"That goon in the back with the gun, he's ex-military and harmless to nice folks like you," Indigo said. "He says it was a high-altitude nuclear blast meant to stop the machines. It's a double-edged sword, though, in that it also takes out the city's power."

"When are they going to fix it?" the wife asked.

"When you say 'they,' who are you referring to?" Cincinnati said, although it was more a rhetorical question than an answer.

The wife looked at the husband, who didn't have an answer, then she looked back at Cincinnati and said, "I don't know."

"Neither do we. We're assuming this is a regional problem, not just a local one."

"Is that why there hasn't been help?" the husband asked.

"Yes," Cincinnati said.

Indigo made no mention of the National Guard and their meat wagons. When there were no more questions, Indigo thanked them again, put the car in gear and continued up the road.

"Those people are screwed," Indigo said. No one objected. Looking in the rear view mirror, her eyes meeting Stanton's, she said, "You were some stock broker hot shot or something, right?"

"I did alright," he said.

"So you talked for a living, right?"

"Yes."

"So why are you so quiet all the time?" she asked, feeling Cincinnati suddenly going very still. She looked at Cincinnati and said, "It's a legitimate question."

"Because it feels good to let everyone else do the talking for a change," he replied.

"We're going to need a leader at some point in time," Indigo said.

"You nominating me?"

"No. Not at all. Leaders get involved. They speak and take charge."

"He led us out of hell," Macy said. "He killed two guys threatening us and an—"

"That's enough, Macy," her mother said.

Macy fell quiet.

"Well it's good to know you've already crossed that line," she said. "That means if it comes to it again, you won't hesitate to do what's necessary."

"This is a community event," Stanton said, "not some shoot out at high noon."

"You don't know that," she said. "I mean, most likely it's just a gathering, but on the off chance that something will happen..."

"I'm ready," he said.

"He stays ready so he doesn't have to get ready," Macy said, which caused a small laugh in Atlanta.

"Holy crap, did you just laugh?" she asked the blonde pixie.

"That was so stupid sounding it was funny," she mused. This, of course, caused Macy to smile, to laugh even.

Five minutes later, they arrived.

"Finally," Indigo said, putting the car in first and killing the engine.

To their surprise, people were already there. A lot of people. They all got out, Rex said nothing about the carbon monoxide poisoning he was sure to have endured, and overall the people's energy was not bad.

They mingled with the growing crowd in the playground, which was rather large and filling up fast. They said hi to just about everyone, introduced themselves as neighbors living just outside the district that were given a flyer by a local boy handing them out. No one seemed to object to them being there which was a relief. It wasn't like they were eating anyone's food, though, or sitting in someone else's reserved seating.

Across the parking lot sized playground were a pair of buildings. The main school. The walls were done in bright colors, the taller of the two buildings having some sort of ecosystem artwork including the blue sky, various plants, some fish presumably under water and a couple of birds in flight.

About thirty minutes before the gathering was set to formally begin, a Sheriff arrived on foot, weapon at his side and in full uniform. It had been awhile since Indigo had seen law enforcement. Real law enforcement.

When they first met, Rex said gang members had hit a police station near their first stolen home and that they were going door to door robbing people.

"Did you see any of them?" she'd asked. "These gangbangers dressed like cops?"

At the time, Indigo asked Rex this question when they were walking back from the field where Indigo first encountered them. The field where members of The Ophidian Horde had taken Rex hostage and threatened the family.

"Who do you think cracked Stanton there on the noggin?" Rex replied.

"So what happened to them? These thugs posing as cops?"

"Cincinnati and I killed them."

It was hard to imagine Cincinnati killing anyone, but she supposed that when it came to saving your family, especially your husband or your daughter, you'd do whatever it took.

Thinking about that, she realized how much she'd been missing her dad. Even her mom. But not her new husband, Tad. Not even a little bit.

The Sheriff was an affable looking man, mid-forties, a cop's build but not in shape. He wore the mustache, sported the little pot belly, walked with his hand resting on the heel of his holstered duty weapon. Indigo wondered if he'd even used it since all this began. When he passed by her, he smiled, but his eyes told her the whole story. There were no ghosts in there.

He hadn't killed anyone.

"You ready?" Rex asked her, even though she was all eyes on the Sheriff.

"Yeah," she said. Indigo looked at Cincinnati who was looking at Stanton; Stanton was looking at Indigo; Macy and Atlanta were talking.

Looking back at Rex, she said, "You feel okay about this?"

"So far, yes. You?"

"So far."

Cincinnati hung back with Stanton and Atlanta. Macy moved toward Rex and Indigo, then gave her mother one last look.

Macy had her pistol tucked into the waist of her jeans under a baby blue man's button-up she borrowed from the closet in her parent's new bedroom.

Indigo had a pistol, too, plus her knives; Rex left the shotgun in the car, but he was strapped, too. When they left to go inside, Cincinnati, Stanton and Atlanta returned to the car to get the guns and find a watchtower point.

Indigo headed toward the buildings with Rex and Macy in

tow. They followed the crowd of families in between the two buildings under a metal awning that stretched the length of the building. A double set of doors stood open as an unspoken invitation inside.

"This is nice," Macy said.

"Looks old, but new at the same time," Indigo replied. "I like it."

The double doors led to a huge open foyer with decorative linoleum tiles: they were colored in beige, green, yellow, blueish purple and orange, all making a swirling pattern where the center was a red ringed grey circle. The Sheriff stood in the circle. This might have been symbolic to people who cared (she didn't), and everyone was gathered around him. Chairs had been pulled out from every classroom, it seemed, but they were filled, leaving standing room only. There was a lot of white noise, considering how many families were there, but the Sheriff put up his hands and called for everyone's attention.

After a moment the foyer fell to a hush.

On the way in, there had been three other doors further down the way, all of them singles. Three more entrances. Three more exits. She nodded for Rex to check out the hallway that most likely led to the exits; he did as instructed. They had a way of reading each other's signals pretty good in tactical settings that she appreciated. The way it looked, they had nothing to worry about, except maybe a few snotty kids and the mounting body heat which, of course, came with an unsavory scent: the I-haven't-showered-in-a-few-days scent.

Rex returned a moment later and tilted his head enough to beckon her. She tapped Macy on the shoulder and the two of them moved to the back of the crowd, closer to Rex. The holes they left behind filled quickly with other people wanting to hear what the Sheriff was saying.

He was talking about the situation being critical without an end in sight. He said the National Guard was here to help, that they were working on restoring the power. To Indigo, it didn't seem like they had any plans of working on the power any time soon, but maybe she had been wrong. She looked at Rex, who was frowning, too.

"Is this an EMP that did this?" a woman asked from the other side of the room.

"We believe so, yes," the Sheriff said, "but we can't be sure the size or the scope of the problem. It could be a west coast problem, or it could be a North American problem. All we know is that calm heads will prevail."

For the next thirty minutes the temperature rose along with the stench of the unwashed masses. People were sweating, Indigo included. This really was a community meeting, but it was a good community that was producing some good ideas for safety and social gatherings to find out who needed help and how they could rally around each other.

That was about when the shooting started.

# CHAPTER TWENTY-THREE

Stanton was on high ground, a raised 7th Street porch of something like fourteen or fifteen steps with a clear view of the playground and one entry point to the school. Stanton didn't expect anything to happen, but since he and Cincinnati had split up, he was there alone and she was watching the 6th Street entrance with Atlanta.

Both girls had the look like they were ready. He hoped it wouldn't come to that, and he was pretty sure it wouldn't. So when the pack of seven thugs with bats and chains and guns appeared he practically crapped his pants.

His heart instantly kicked into high gear, nearly blowing a gasket from the burst of pressure. Scampering down the bajillion concrete stairs as quickly and as quietly as he could, he ducked behind an old Mazda Protégé, saw exactly where they were headed and opened fire before they got too close. At this point, he was pretty sure that inside of the next thirty seconds, he'd be dead.

It didn't matter. That's why he fired again.

With so many people to protect, his first shots needed to count. And they did. Both were head shots; both men dropped.

The other five ducked, turned to where he was firing and opened up a can of lead hell.

He ducked down, but the Mazda's glass was breaking everywhere and exit holes were punching through the metal.

One round blew past his face, causing him to scoot as far to the front of the sedan as he could. Two of the seven were down and the other five were coming; he only had to take out one or maybe two more before they got to him, that way he'd make it a fair fight for Rex and Indigo when he was dead.

He said a quick prayer for Sin and Macy, asked God to protect them as he steadied his hand and stood and open-fired like a man.

---

I practically go paralyzed with fear as I see a huge pack of men appear down the street on Balboa. It's even harder for me to breathe when half of them break off and start up 6<sup>th</sup> Street heading straight to for the school.

Could this be a coincidence? I don't think so.

Every single one of them looks hard, their walk aggressive, their bodies loaded down with weapons.

Pushing Atlanta behind me, we duck inside the pocketed alcove of a grey, three story residence with teal painted trim around the windows. We can hide inside here, but we'll only last for so long if something goes down. I try the door handle, but it's locked. We're screwed. If we're caught in here, we're dead. Or worse.

"Cincinnati?" Atlanta asks. She doesn't see what I see, but she sees the expression on my face and it's enough to startle her.

"Get your gun ready," I tell her with too much adrenaline in my voice. "You can shoot that thing, can't you?"

"Yes."

"Can you aim, too?"

"If you get me close enough. What's happening?"

Stealing a quick breath, I pop my head around the corner, see eight of them closing in on us. Do I shoot now, or do I let them get inside and try to trap them there? With a bunch of families, my daughter and my brother inside, the answer is clear.

"When they head up the stairs," I tell Atlanta, "the second their backs are too us, we start shooting. Got it?"

All the blood leaves her face, but she nods yes.

"We miss, we die," I tell her.

Atlanta nods again, her face as terrified as any I've ever seen, and that's saying something.

Before the gang heads inside, they gather in a circle and game plan. With my stomach in my throat and my bowels milliseconds from emptying out against my will, I grip my gun too tight. Trying to control my breathing, hearing them talking about heading inside and mowing down all the men and children, I wipe my sweaty palms on my jeans, not once taking my eyes off the group.

The fact that they're talking about killing children sets my blood on fire.

Over my shoulder, I say, "I go, you go. Got it?"

"Got it," Atlanta says.

Before I can go, the shooting starts. It sounds like it's coming from the other side of the school. *Stanton.* The pack of thugs all startle, then turn toward the sound of gunfire. The second they're moving on the school, I burst out of the alcove and start firing. Behind me Atlanta does the same thing. We hit five of the eight, but the remaining three scramble for cover and I'm clicking an empty magazine.

Atlanta is doing the same.

We both scurry back into the alcove, realizing our mistake the second we make it. The alcove is a trap. Gunshots ring out, slamming into the stucco walls and the wood and glass front doors. If they're broken out, we can get inside, but by the rate of fire, we won't have time and we'd probably get cut pretty badly by the broken glass if we tried.

"Are you hit?" I ask Atlanta.

"No."

"Are you reloading?"

"Yes."

I eject the magazine the way Stanton and Rex taught me, replace it with the spare in my back pocket.

"Ready?" I ask.

"Go."

Outside gunfire is still erupting the next street over, but on our side, there's only silence. There are three left, and we didn't hit any of them, so I take it to mean they've either fled or they're coming up on—

I see him almost too late. His head pops around the corner and our eyes meet. I freeze, but Atlanta doesn't. The sound of the weapon discharging in such a tight, enclosed space sends my ears ringing. I didn't realize I'd cried out until it was too late.

A wash of red blows out the back of the thug's head and he drops to the ground. More gunfire pocks and peppers the alcove, but I can't hear it over the piercing ring in my ears.

Atlanta had no choice but to fire right beside my ear. I get that. Still, it's got me feeling a bit wobbly. Holding my hands over my hears, I step backwards into the alcove's pocket. Atlanta steps forward.

When I see the two men, I know it's all over, but Atlanta starts shooting anyway, both of them ducking and firing at the same time. But not Atlanta. She just stands there in a shooter's position emptying her magazine in an attempt to take out these two clowns.

---

Inside the school, the gunfire gets everyone in a stir. The Sheriff immediately tells everyone to stay calm as he takes out his weapon and moves toward the doors.

"What's going on, Sheriff?" Rex asked, moving up next to the law man.

"Stand back, son."

Rex heard the shooting coming from both sides of the school and suddenly he knew what was happening.

"They're flanking us," Rex said. "You'd know that if you brought reinforcements, but you didn't."

"Those your people? The ones firing back?"

"Yes."

He looked down his nose at Rex and said, "I said stand back. Now."

Rex put his hands up and moved back, turning to give Indigo the signal. As he was turning, automatic gunfire lit up the large foyer and people started to drop, the Sheriff first. Rex pushed and shoved his way toward Indigo and Macy.

"Follow me," he yelled over the screaming. Indigo was ready, but Macy was looking terrified. He slapped her in the face hard and said, "Get it together!"

She came to, sprung into action.

They headed for one of the three northern exits just as a gunman entered from the west end of the foyer and started unloading what sounded like a bump-stock AR into the crowd.

When they burst through the door, Rex and Indigo saw the guy outside lighting up the west end of the foyer through the open doors. Indigo shot him in the ribs. He fired off two retaliatory rounds that had all three of them diving for cover.

Macy was freezing up, fear all over her face, her hands shaking.

The gunman stopped firing when his injuries overtook him. They couldn't do anything about the shooter inside, but on either side of the school gun battles were waging. Out on 7th, it looked like Stanton was pinned down by a single shooter. On the other side of the school, 6th Street, his sister and Atlanta were taking fire.

Cincinnati or Stanton?

"I'll get the girls," Indigo said. "Macy you stay here and cover us, just in case."

Indigo rushed down the outdoor hallway toward 6$^{th}$ and he ran for Stanton on 7$^{th}$. He broke out into the playground with no cover and only a prayer for protection.

The guys going after Stanton were big, both of them rounding the hood of a shot-to-hell Mazda. One of them had a baseball bat; but the lead had a shotgun at the ready. There were bodies laid out on the pavement everywhere.

Stanton had to be behind the Mazda. He was either trapped or dead. That's when he saw Stanton on bent knees working his way around the trunk of the car, opposite his attackers.

Rex didn't exactly heave a sigh of relief as much as he put on the speed. He was within twenty feet when the guy with the shotgun turned and saw Rex. It was just a matter of time. He spun the weapon on Rex around the same time Stanton saw the guy turn. The shotgun went off right after Stanton put a round through the side of his head. The big guy fell over and Stanton ran toward Rex firing on the guy with the bat. He dropped and Rex yelled, "The girls are under attack!"

Rex turned and ran back for Cincinnati. Stanton took chase and was closing in on him more quickly than expected.

---

Macy couldn't just cower there while a shooter was inside killing all those people. Swallowing hard, she got up, crept back into the building the way they'd come out.

Sniffling, pawing the tears from her eyes, she said, "Get it together. Do your part."

She made her way back into the building, hurrying to the sounds of automatic gunfire. When she got to the small hallway that turned right and opened up to the foyer, she smelled gunpowder and blood.

Horrified, she stilled herself, fought the upsurge of her stomach.

When she peeked around the corner, four women were huddled in the corner, bawling and shaking. One of them was crawling toward her child. This was the woman they'd asked for directions from. All her daughters and her husband were dead.

Everyone was dead.

A rough jolt of nausea hit her as she saw the shooter packing an extended magazine into his assault rifle. She walked into the foyer and opened fire. Nine rounds, every single one of them missing the intended target.

Her heart dropped. Startled, the shooter quickly checked himself over, then realized he wasn't hit. His fear became a sadistic smile as he dropped the AR, grabbed his pistol and emptied the magazine in her direction.

------

Atlanta's out of ammo and I can't hear anything but the punch of every shot making my ears ring extra sharp.

The minute Atlanta clicks empty, the two guys get to their feet and break out a pair of automatic weapons. I say a brief prayer to God, ask Him to watch over Macy, Stanton and Rex because—by the look of things—I'm not going to make it. The barrage of gunfire is cut short by the sound of an over-revved engine. The shooters don't see the rusted white Jeep bearing down on them, but the second they hear it, it's already too late.

The Jeep plows into the pair, smashing the front hood and sending both guys flying through the air. Atlanta steps out of the alcove and drags me with her. We both see the Jeep's bloody hood with relief. Then we see Indigo. She's rushing down the stairs, heading toward the men lying broken in the road.

The driver gets out of the Jeep. He's a young kid, good looking and scared. He did this on purpose, though, so maybe he wasn't that scared.

My equilibrium not being what it needs to be, I grab a parked car's hood to keep from falling over. I pull back my hand and see red on the palm, from where I'd been plugging my damaged ear. Suddenly I'm worried I won't ever hear right again.

"Are you two okay?" the kid asks both me and Atlanta.

I nod my head and say, "Ears ringing," too loud. I hear myself, but I sound like I'm underwater.

Looking up, I watch Indigo put bullets into the hearts of both shooters, just to make sure.

"Jesus," the kid is saying. He's got a nasty red line on his head. It looks like a cut, but longer, deeper. His face also has a bunch of little cuts, which look a few days old.

Indigo jogs to us and sees the tremors in my eyes. She looks at the kid, who's standing there not knowing how he can help, and I see Atlanta telling her what happened, that she shot too close to my ear.

They both look at me and say, "Stay here," and I nod my head, sitting down on the sidewalk and feeling like run over crap.

The kid watches Atlanta and Indigo head back inside the school. He looks down at me not knowing what to do. Finally he extends his hand. I take it and he helps me up. He waves for me to follow him, and I do.

I know what he's doing.

He walks me to the Jeep, opens the passenger door and helps me inside. This old thing isn't nearly comfortable, but it's a heck of a lot better than sitting on the sidewalk. He runs around the other side and gets a bottle of water and an old shirt.

Back with me, he balls up and wets the shirt, then gently dabs at the soft skin under my ear. I'm looking at him and he's saying, "Can you hear me?"

"A little," I say too loud.

He glances over to where the girls ran back to the school, like maybe he heard something. To me it sounds like the muffled, far-away sounds of more gunfire. Putting myself aside for a minute, I start to worry about the others.

"What's your name?" I ask.

The boy turns around and says, "Hagan. Hagan Justus."

"Thank you, Hagan," I manage to tell him. "I think you saved our lives."

---

The second the guy starts shooting, Rex runs through the open door squeezing the trigger of his own gun. The gun is jammed though, a round sitting wrong in the chamber. He goes with it though, running faster and spinning the weapon in his hand. The shooter sees him and turns the weapon on Rex, but it's too late. Rex slams butt of his weapon into the guy, pistol whipping the hell out of the side of his head.

They both go to the ground, the shooter out cold.

Rex sees four women in a corner, huddling together, a mass of dead bodies—men, women and children alike—and his niece, Macy. She's laid out on the floor, her blonde hair fanned out behind her.

"Oh, God," he says, scrambling to his feet and moving through the sea of bodies toward her. He slips twice in ponds of blood, but manages to not fall.

Stanton is right behind him screaming Macy's name.

His niece has two blooms of red on her: one above her left breast, another on her shoulder, plus her ear is nicked, a chunk of the skin just gone from where the bullet took it.

He checks her pulse.

It's weak.

"Macy," Rex said, holding back the rage, the terror, the tears. "Macy, honey. Wake up for me baby, please. Please just wake up."

Suddenly kneeling down beside him, Stanton's going to pieces.

Rex tapped her face, said her name again, garnered no response. Stanton is touching her, pumping her hand, saying "No, no, no," over and over again and a sad, mewling rush. He finally pushes Rex aside just as Indigo and Atlanta burst through the foyer's main doors.

*This is my fault,* Rex was thinking to himself. He shouldn't have pushed her. If he hadn't have pushed her, hit her, she might have stayed put instead of coming in here.

*What was she thinking?!*

Indigo saw Macy, hurried over and knelt down, the concern bare in her eyes. Atlanta saw her, walked over at a slower, more shocked pace, then hovered over them for a second. Stanton was holding Macy. He was sobbing, crying out her name. Rex looked up at Atlanta, saw her eyes taking in the carnage. Then he saw those same eyes find the shooter.

Saying nothing, she walked over to him, aimed her pistol at his face and pulled the trigger. The chamber clicked empty. She squeezed the trigger seven more times before Indigo said, "Atlanta, stop."

She reached down and picked up the man's AR instead. Looking at the weapon, she pushed in the magazine and aimed the weapon at the man's head.

"Atlanta, no!" Indigo shouted.

At that point, Rex had no idea why Indigo wanted to stop her. He wanted the girl to empty fifty rounds into that son of a bitch for what he's done to Macy, to this community.

Atlanta ignored Indigo, so Indigo fired her weapon into the ceiling, jolting Atlanta (and all of us) out of her haze.

She turned and looked back at Indigo.

"We need him alive," Indigo said. "Alive."

"He doesn't deserve life," she replied, tears standing in her eyes, her cheeks bone white. "Not after this."

"He'll deserve what we do to him, that I promise you. Now find me some water and a clean cloth. Macy's been shot and we need to help her."

The guy was stirring at her feet, which got Indigo to her feet. Atlanta saw this, though, so she cracked him in the head with the stock of his own weapon. The shooter's head flopped back down. Atlanta reeled up and struck him again, harder this time.

Rex expected her to go for a third time, but she didn't. She headed back to them, side stepping the bodies, then handed Rex the gun.

"Thanks," he said.

She didn't say anything.

Instead, she turned and looked around, scanning the bodies until she found what she was looking for. A tipped over bottle of water, the top shot open.

Stanton looked at Indigo and said, "Knife," to which she handed him one of her knives. He cut away the sleeve of his own shirt, then took it and the bottle of water and handed it to Indigo.

"My sister's an ER nurse," Rex said. "She can help. We just need to get her in here."

"She might have a blown-out ear drum," Indigo said, not looking at him.

"She's okay otherwise?"

"Pay attention, Rex." She glanced up at him with that look, the one of extreme seriousness. "If we don't help her, she could die."

"I'm focused," he said, handing her back her knife.

"Good, because I need you to read her pulse for me. If she's got a sucking wound in her chest, we're going to need to sit her up. And Stanton, you need to hold her hand and talk to her. She needs to hear your voice."

Rex moved around Indigo, to the top of Macy's head, brushed her hair out of the way and sat down where he could take her pulse at her neck.

He started counting.

Stanton took her hand and began talking to her, telling her she was going to be alright, that she was terribly brave and needed to be brave just a little bit longer while her friends work on her. He had two fingers on her wrist, checking her pulse, too.

Indigo cut away part of the girl's shirt, pulling it back to her bra. The first wound was obvious, a single crimson-black entry wound just above her breast. There was a blood blossom around it from where blood had seeped into the shirt and bloomed on her ivory white skin.

Indigo watched it for a second, then said, "It's not a sucking wound. It's damn close to the danger zone, but she lucked out. Rex, what's the pulse?"

He told her. Stanton nodded his head, too.

It was stronger than he thought, which meant she might not have internal bleeding. But she wasn't out of the woods yet. Who knew what kind of damage the bullet had done to the nerves and arteries clustered inside her?

"The shoulder wound is clean," Indigo said, "but it's high, so depending on the trajectory of the wound, she might have a nicked or broken scapula."

"What makes you think that?" Rex asked, not sure how she knew what she did, but glad she did.

"The close proximity to the spine of the scapula. If we're lucky, it will have passed through the muscle. We need to turn her over. Stanton, let's bring her arms in to her side. I need to keep her stabilized in case there's a neck injury from the fall, but I need to see her back, too."

On her count, they turned Macy on her side enough for Indigo to pull her shirt off her back and see the exit wound. The shot came out clean, fairly straight entry and exit points.

"Okay," she said. Gently, they laid her back down. Looking at Rex, she said, "I need your other sleeve. We need to wash the wounds first, then apply some clean cloth to it. We need the wounds to clot. Your sister can take it from there." To Atlanta, she said, "I need you to find the infirmary in this place. Locate some bandages and some medical tape—or even sports tape—if you can. And hurry."

Rex glanced up at Atlanta, then nodded to the shooter's

weapon. Understanding that he wanted her armed, she picked it up, then hurried off.

For the next few minutes, Indigo washed the wounds and dressed them as best as she could with the squares of Rex's cotton sleeves. To Stanton and Rex, she said, "We need to keep light pressure on these wounds for the next ten minutes. Stanton, I need you to really lean on that wound. If it seems you're leaning a little too hard, that's just the right pressure."

"Where are you going?" Rex asked.

Saying nothing, she got up, walked through the dead bodies, past the women grieving over their loved ones, then to the shooter. He wasn't coming to, so Indigo knelt down, rolled him over and slapped his face twice, really hard.

---

The shooter was a junkie at best. He was too thin, had cold sores on his lip and tats all the way up to his jaw. The tats on display told her he was hard, that he wasn't aching to get a nine-to-five job. That was no surprise. Neither was the ink he wore. It was similar to the other gangbangers she'd ended.

After being hit, he started to stir.

Good.

Before he could protest, she pulled out her knife and cut the front of his shirt in half. He began to squirm, but it was too late. She was looking at a chest painted with tattoos. She didn't care about ninety-nine percent of them, only *the one*. The large black snake coiled over the words, The Ophidian Horde.

"Son of a—"

He tried to focus his eyes as he was coming to. Indigo straddled his chest, planted her knees on his biceps, pinning him down. He groaned, writhed and finally came around.

The curse words began to roll, sloppy and weak at first, but then more forceful.

"I kept you alive for a reason," Indigo said. "See, you're going to be the messenger."

And with that, she leaned forward, the bulk of her weight pressing down on his arms so hard he snarled and fought her. A second later he stopped fighting. Rather, the fight in him changed. She snuck a look over her shoulder and saw two of the four ladies holding down his legs.

"Hurt him," one of them said with tear soaked eyes, a red nose and rosy cheeks made flush from a deep, personal agony.

Turning back around, her eyes changing, things going dark along the edges, she used her left hand to pin down his head, then she used her right hand and the knife to carve the word INDIGO across his forehead in large, jagged letters.

The wild screaming bothered her at first, as did the blood; she wouldn't be deterred though. Clearing her head, she worked to ignore his ruckus, and every so often, she'd swipe away the blood so she could see what she was doing.

When she was done, he'd been reduced to a blubbering mess. Using her sleeve, she wiped away the rest of the blood, studied her handiwork, then said, "You're free to go. But if I see you again, I'll kill you on the spot, no questions asked. Got it?"

He nodded.

She got off him, stood up, then sheathed her knife at her side. The woman they'd gotten directions from earlier, the mother of three, she walked up and hugged Indigo. She just grabbed her and pulled her in close, holding her so tight Indigo could feel that ragged clamoring of her heart.

"Thank you," she said.

And with that, she yanked Indigo's knife free of its sheath, ran to the shooter as he was getting up, then fell into a screaming/stabbing fit of such fury Indigo dared not get involved. Everyone stopped to watch her, disbelief rocking each of them.

By the time the woman was done, the shooter had been stabbed some fifty or sixty times. He was drenched red from throat to belt. The woman was so exhausted she couldn't even lift her hand anymore. She could barely even hold the knife.

Indigo went to her, touched her shoulder, causing the woman to flinch ever so slightly.

"It's okay," she said. The knife fell from the woman's hand. Indigo picked it up, wiped it clean on her pants, then sheathed it, pulling her shirt over it so no one else could grab it.

The woman just sat there, sobbing, wailing. The other women came to her, helped her to her feet, held her closely.

Atlanta appeared just then with what looked like a small med kit.

No one said a thing about the woman's rage, and even though all of them were shocked by the widow's madness, none of them were surprised in the slightest.

"I got medical tape," Atlanta said, breaking the silence.

By then, Macy was coming to. Her eyes bobbed open, but they didn't stay open. Her mouth twitched, then her face contorted in pain and she began to cry. Rex took over putting pressure on her wound while Stanton held her hand, reassured her that she was okay.

Indigo moved Rex aside, then pulled off the blood-soaked patches of cotton, dried the surrounding areas and applied a large bandage. They did this front and back despite Macy's profuse crying.

Indigo looked up and saw Stanton quietly crying, too. This almost broke Indigo's heart, but she wouldn't let it. She couldn't break down now.

"Macy," she said. "Macy." The girl's crying died down a bit and Indigo said, "Can you move your neck without pain?"

"Everything hurts," she blubbered.

"I know, sweetheart, but I need you to try very, very slowly, and tell me if you feel anything strange."

The girl moved her head from left to right, then said, "No."

"Good. Now I'm going to tell you what's going on because

you're a strong girl, one of the toughest I've met. Can you listen to me? Focus on the words I'm saying?"

She stopped crying altogether, then gave a brief nod and tried to open her eyes.

"You've been shot, but you must be the luckiest girl in the world because the bullets went through you and it seems they missed your vital organs."

"I can't feel my right arm," she said. "It's...numb."

"You have a lot of nerves near your armpit, so it's going to feel like that for awhile. First though, we have to get you to your mother so she can look at you and take care of you."

They waited for a second before she said, "Okay."

With her eyes open, Stanton and Macy helped lift her to her feet, each and every move sending shockwaves of pain through the girl. To her credit, she didn't cry out or protest, even though fresh tears were streaming down her cheeks.

"Can you walk?" Indigo asked.

"I think. It's just...I can't feel my right arm."

"It's just nerves," Stanton said again. "You're going to be okay, pumpkin."

"It's a bit of a walk to the car," Indigo said. "You'll be going home with your mother in a different car."

"Why?" she said.

"It's easier to get into and it's a lot closer. Plus your mom is there now. She might have a burst ear drum, so she's not hearing so well. She'll want to see you, though."

They walked her to the Jeep where they were met by the Jeep's driver and a very worried, very unbalanced looking Cincinnati.

When the boy saw Macy, he grew intently focused on her, first her face, then her wounds.

"I need you to take us home," Indigo said to him. "Can you do that?"

"Yes," he replied. Then: "But I need something from you." He was looking down at the medical kit. When he looked up, he said, "Someone blew up our home. The roof collapsed on my mother. She might be dying."

Indigo's heart skipped a beat or two. This kid just rescued them and was willing to help while his mother lie dying in a collapsed house.

"We live ten minutes from here," Indigo told him. "I have medical supplies at my house, so we can get her the help she needs. Are you okay with that?"

He nodded his head.

"Good, let's go." When they got in the Jeep, she said, "By the way, who are you?"

"Hagan Justus, son of Lenna and Jagger Justus."

"Are you famous or something?" she asked.

"No. I'm just telling you their names in case I die unexpectedly. That way you'll know who to contact if things are ever right again."

"Is he here, in the city? Your dad?"

"No. He's military. He was in Corpus Christi, Texas when all this went down. He's in Camp Pendleton now. But he could be dead, too. He never got home."

"My dad was in San Diego also," she said, holding his eye. "He never made it home either."

# CHAPTER TWENTY-FOUR

Back at her house a few minutes later, Indigo unlocked the front door and headed inside, not expecting to see the man she ran into several nights back when she was robbing a home.

"Rider was it?"

"Good memory, little one," he mused.

Rex and Stanton walked Macy through the door, stopping at the sight of the handsome, older looking gentleman sitting on the couch.

"He's okay," Indigo said. "We know each other."

They walked Macy to the couch. Rider got up to make room for her. They laid Macy down on her back. Cincinnati said she was feeling better, although her hearing was only about fifty percent. Still, that was an improvement from before when she wasn't hearing much of anything.

Cincinnati knelt down next to her daughter and took her pulse.

Everyone looked at her expectantly.

"It's strong."

Still no internal bleeding. Well, most likely no internal bleeding. Cincinnati was the ER nurse, not Indigo. She just remembered what her grandpa taught her about dressing field wounds.

He was a hunter and an archer, just like her. May God bless and nourish his soul.

To Rider, she said, "How'd you get in here?"

He produced a house key, which baffled her considering she held the only key to the house. Well, her and her father.

"I see you're doing alright," he said. "Lots of food, supplies, ammo. You did good, kid."

"I'd be doing a lot better if you weren't in my house right now."

Atlanta, Stanton and Rex were all looking at the guy, wondering if he was going to be trouble. Hagan stepped inside the house and he, too, set eyes on Rider.

"I told you I'd check up on you, but I'm here for other reasons. There's a place we've been preparing. It's where people can come and stay. A compound of sorts. There's a doctor, security detail, some food and plenty of room for all of you. Plus this compound comes with something special," he said, looking right at Indigo.

"Oh and what's that?"

"Me," said a voice from behind her.

She turned and saw her mother standing there and damn near broke into tears.

"Mom?"

Her mother pulled her into a hug. She couldn't believe this was actually happening. Inside she felt her organs beginning to shake.

*This isn't real, is it?*

She drew back from her mother, stared at her and said, "I thought you were dead. I went to your house…"

"You've been to the house?" she asked.

"Yes," she said, so lost in her mother's eyes, she was sure this was all a dream.

"Did you see Tad?"

Reality set in hard and fast. Indigo couldn't look into her eyes when she said, "Yes."

"And?"

"Can we talk about him later? I'm still trying to figure out how you are real, and why you're here with him."

"He saved my life," she said, looking at Rider

"Is this true?" she asked. He gave a humble nod. "Well thank you, Rider."

"You said you have a doctor?" Hagan asked, looking at Rider and not Cincinnati.

"Yes, we do."

"And you're a nurse?" he said, now turning to Cincinnati.

"She is," Rex said for her. "In the ER."

"So between the two of you, do you think my mom will be okay?"

"What's wrong with your mother?" Rider asked. Hagan told him and he said, "It all depends on her injuries."

"So this doctor you have," Indigo asked, "is she any good?"

"Sarah's her name. Doctor Sarah Richards. And yes, she's good."

"You trust her?"

"She's the one who's been caring for me," her mother said, catching Indigo's attention. "So, yes."

"I think it's time you and your friends relocate," Rider said. "Strength in numbers and all that."

"Where to?"

"City college down on Masonic, on the other side of the Panhandle."

"We've been there," Stanton said. "Met a guy in an old Chevy truck with an arsenal in the bed."

"Waylon."

"Nice guy," Stanton replied.

"I can go with Hagan," Rider said, "get his mom and younger brother. But after that, you guys should come with us."

"I'm going to stay here," Indigo said. "Just in case my father comes back."

"Where's he at?" Indigo's mother asked.

"San Diego," Indigo replied. "Sales conference, or something like that."

"Then I'm staying," her mother announced. "If that's okay with you."

She held her mother's eyes, then slowly nodded her head and said, "It is."

# CHAPTER TWENTY-FIVE

The former hitman and new head of The Ophidian Horde sat comfortably at his desk deep inside the half-destroyed Sutter Medical building reading his Bible under the light of an open window. A knock at the door pulled him from this brief utopia, but he didn't stop reading until he'd finished his passage. After that, he closed the book and said, "Come in."

Gunderson, his chief enforcer, entered with a black garbage bag in hand. "What can I do for you?"

"Chandler Diggs and his boys learned of a community meeting in Balboa Hollow—it's just above the park on 8th and Fulton—"

"I'm familiar with the area," he said, his eyes dipping to the bag he had in hand. "I don't know this Chandler Diggs though."

"He's a convert. Goes by the name Blood Pig."

The hitman gave a nod of recognition, allowing Gunderson to continue. "They were slaughtered a few days back. A former soldier of his went looking for them. Found a massacre."

"A massacre? Who'd they find, besides Blood Pig?"

"There was a community meeting. I sent Chandler and his men to handle it, per your orders."

"So the community killed them?"

"That's what's unsettling, sir. Everyone's dead. Chandler, his men, fifty or sixty members of the community. It's a blood bath."

"Where at?"

"Frank McCoppin Elementary, on 6$^{th}$ and Balboa."

The hitman frowned, truly disturbed. He went to Frank McCoppin as a kid. Before he became...what he became...he was just a boy and that school held many fine memories for him.

"Who did this? And why wasn't I told you were moving on the elementary school?"

"You said handle it, sir. So I handled it. From this point forward, I'll be sure to apprise you of all movements in detail. We've got several more planned over the next few days, but..."

"But what?"

"This one gives me pause," Gunderson said.

"Stop sounding so formal for Christ's sake. I'm not going to shoot you for lack of manners or an improper usage of the English language." Then: "What's in the bag?"

Gunderson sat the bag on a chair facing the hitman's desk, reached inside, fidgeted a little, then hauled out a decapitated head by the nostrils, almost like it was a bowling ball and not attached to a body a few days ago.

"What does that say? On his head? Indigo?" He studied the head, then looked up and said, "What the hell is 'Indigo?'"

"We think it's a name," Gunderson replied, "but it could be a new faction, too."

"So they cut his head off?"

"I cut his head off."

"Why would you do that?"

"His body was turned into a pin cushion in the worst way. Besides, it was easier to bring him to you like this rather than drag back an entire body. I can retrieve the rest of him if you want."

"No, but I do want you to go back and burn the bodies. All of them. Burn the school down, too."

"There are houses all around the school, sir."

"And if they burn?" the former hitman asked, raising his voice, perturbed. "If this whole city burns? What will be the difference from now?"

Gunderson lowered his head, humbled.

"You did good, Gunderson," he said, his calm returning. "I see now that I was right about you. You're going to make a fine enforcer."

"Thank you, sir."

Reaching his hand out, he said, "Let me have him."

Pulling his fingers out of Blood Pig's nostrils, he handed the head over, setting it on the desk on the bloody flat of the cut-off neck.

"Not on the desk," he said, sliding the Bible over. "Use a coaster."

Hesitating, Gunderson set the man's head down on the Bible, steadying it, then standing back while the hitman looked it over.

The self-appointed leader of The Ophidian Horde turned the head so he was eye to eye with it. Then: "This Indigo, whatever it is...a gang, a person...whatever, apparently this was some form of retaliation."

"We believe so, too."

"Gunderson, your first order of business on this sad day is to find out who or what Indigo is, and then report back. I'd like to head up the matter myself when the time comes."

"Yes, sir."

Making a fist and popping his knuckles, he looked at his chief enforcer with the deadest of gazes and said, "We're literally going to rip the spine out of this Indigo thing and hang it from the nearest lamppost so people know who we are, and what we're capable of."

"Indeed, sir."

"Good," he said. "Now get on it."

END OF BOOK 3


SNEAK PEEK OF *THE INFERNAL REGIONS...*

# THE INFERNAL REGIONS: CHAPTER 1

*The Day of the Attack. Corpus Christi, TX.*

First Lieutenant Jagger Justus and Second Lieutenant Camila Cardoza checked into the Naval Air Station Corpus Christi, otherwise known as NAS Corpus Christi, for advance flight training. The two marines were bunking in separate quarters, but Jagger knew Camila wished they were bunking together. She'd always been a touch sweet on him, which she made no bones about, even though he was eight years her senior and married with two boys.

Camila once told him that as early as fifteen, she'd been attracted to older men, her father's best friend specifically. She'd said, "You're not that old, and I'm not that young..." to which he always replied, "I'm too married for you. This has nothing to do with age."

Jagger settled into his quarters, having laid down for only a few minutes before Camila came knocking on his door.

He opened his eyes, drew a breath. "Come in," he said, stretched out on his bunk, fingers laced behind his head. He'd been hoping for a little shut eye, a power nap at best.

The twenty-five year old Guatemalan firecracker stepped

inside his quarters and said, "I don't know about you, but I'm ready for a sit down at either the Oasis Tavern, Circle R Mexican or the Boardwalk Café." She was in fatigues and a green t-shirt. The t-shirt was too tight, as usual. She wasn't a busty woman, but the girl knew the effect her body had on a man and wasn't afraid to boast.

He looked away, even though it was clear she preferred he didn't. He wasn't about to be rude or send the wrong message.

"I'm down for the Oasis, so long as you have some dignity about yourself in there. You know that place can draw an unsavory crowd."

"That was last time," she said. "Besides, I have you to protect me, so..."

Sitting up, planting both feet on the ground, he said, "Like you can't protect yourself." She gave a slight shrug of the shoulders, coupled with a sly, sexy smile. Looking away, he said, "I'll find us a ride."

"Did I ever tell you how much I adore your resourcefulness?" she teased.

There was something about her accent that complimented her look, giving off the impression that she was an innocent twenty-something when really she could go toe to toe with guys twice her size. She'd say it was because she had brothers. The truth was, this slender little fighting machine had been doing kickboxing since she was six.

Rolling his eyes, he said, "C'mon Cardoza, we just got here." He didn't mind the subtle flirtation here and there, but lately she'd been pouring it on.

"What?" she asked, feigning virtue. "I'm just excited to earn my hours, aren't you? I mean, what's sexier than Tilt Rotor training in Texas? Meet you back here in ten?"

"So *I'm* arranging the ride?" he asked.

"Didn't we already talk about this?" she said on the way out, giving him a wink and leaving the door open.

He stood and shut the door, wondering how the hell she

could go from steadfast to flirty then back to professional, all in under a minute. What drove a woman like Camila was a mystery for sure, one that left him wondering why she'd been so forward lately. He knew Camila left her boyfriend last month, but he didn't know why. Jagger suspected he'd cheated, but Camila never let on. Twice this past week he found her crying. Once he made the mistake of hugging her at her most vulnerable point. The way she settled into him was too comfortable. It made it easy to see himself being with a woman like her, but he wouldn't act on it. He couldn't. Now, contemplating the idea of throwing back drinks with her several states away from home, he longed to be back with Lenna and the boys.

Drawing out a long sigh, he stretched, then jumped on the phone and arranged a vehicle. Deep down he was attracted to his co-pilot, to the way she pined after him, to the way she looked at him and tried to get with him in spite of his commitment to Lenna. He hated admitting this to himself, but it was true. Still, he sought to live a upright life, even though she'd somehow turned this into a flirtationship she often said she enjoyed.

There was more though. More truth to her behavior than he wanted to acknowledge. She'd do anything he wanted her to do, no matter what, when or where—he needed only say the word. He would never say that word...

The knock on his door startled him out of his reverie and he brought himself to attention. He pulled open the door and there she was.

"You get us a ride, Lt?"

"Sure did."

Moments later their ride arrived. Jagger was handed the keys to a Jeep, but he looked at Camila and asked if she wanted to drive.

"You should drive me," she said. "I'm a traditionalist."

A half-hearted laugh escaped him and he said, "Yeah, right," which caused her to blush a little and bat her eyelashes at him.

She really was very cute, completely disarming.

They drove off base to the Oasis Tavern, pulled up two stools and ordered drinks. The atmosphere was on the dim side, the county music upbeat but not too rowdy, the crowd surprisingly well behaved. There were only about a dozen patrons, most of them hardened men, but not rough looking. He and Camila were on their third drink when the peninsula was first bombed.

"Did you hear that?" Jagger asked. He was looking over at Camila and straining to hear above the din of a Chris Stapleton country song.

A second, third and fourth concussion sounded, sending tremors through the ground and startling them all. Camila's eyes widened with concern.

"Turn the music down!" Jagger told the bartender. "Everyone be quiet!"

The mood of the bar shifted on a dime. A look of alarm broke over the surface of the bartender's otherwise neutral face as he killed the music. Everyone sat on edge, silent, listening intently.

When the next bomb hit, Jagger kicked off his stool and was first out the door with his Camila on his heels. Everyone else poured out after them and in seconds all eyes were locked on the horizon.

"My God," Jagger heard himself say as several columns of smoke rose into the clear blue sky. Fishing his keys out of his pocket, moving toward their ride, he said, "C'mon Cardoza!"

They jumped into the Jeep they'd borrowed and raced up NAS Drive toward what looked like a slew of explosions. A fleet of drones zipped overhead, causing them both to look up.

"Are those ours?" Camila asked loudly.

"Not sure," he answered over the heady reverberation of the engine.

Jagger blew past a row of crappy looking restaurants and used car dealerships, past a storage lot and half a dozen low-slung buildings you'd never see in *Architectural Digest,* unless they had the Trailer Park Edition. Twice they roared past slower vehicles on the wrong side of the road causing Camila to stop breathing as she grabbed ahold of something, anything.

When they approached NAS's front gate, he told Camila to hold on. Never even touching the brakes, he swung into oncoming traffic and bypassed the base's gate shack completely. Minutes later the NEX gas station was hit. It went up in a series of explosions that sent fire and rolling smoke into the sky.

The concussion waves rocked their Jeep on its springs. More drones flew by, breaking formation a second later. Artillery fire from further out sliced through the air, wobbling and then downing several drones.

"There must be thirty of them!" Camila screamed, leaning forward and peering up through the dusty windshield.

"Keep it together, Cardoza!" he said, his own teeth set on edge.

"Are you kidding me?" she asked, glaring at him.

He had to admit, the woman was pretty chill under fire. Was he though? They were finding out by the second.

By the time Lexington Blvd dead-ended at Ocean Blvd, the Navy Marine Corps Relief Society building had been leveled, as well as the Naval Exchange, the Post Office and the Navy Legal Assistance Office.

A quick flick of the eyes into his rear view mirror showed him a drone bearing down on them. He jerked the wheel at the last minute, causing the tires to screech and yelp in protest. The inside tires lifted off the ground putting them on two wheels and slightly out of control. Gritting his teeth, Jagger held on. A line of gunfire pocked the road in front of them, spitting up bits of asphalt and gravel as the drone rocketed overhead. He ripped the wheel back around and managed to keep them from toppling over.

"Did that thing just shoot at us?!" Camila screamed, obviously shaken. Jagger was too rattled to tell her that luck alone just saved their lives.

With the exploding sounds of violence and warfare upon

them, Jagger pushed the Jeep harder, forcing himself not to rationalize what was going on, to just *move*. He kept his foot on the gas. He drew a hard left on Ocean, the back end breaking loose in a baying squeal. They shot past a pair of Tilt-Rotor Valor's sitting on the tarmac in smoking ruin before veering too quickly into Hangar 46. Jagger flew into the hangar, stood on the brakes and slid sideways to a stop.

They were now in the heart of the defensive operation.

At least two dozen men were moving about the hangar with purpose, although it would look like frenzy to any civilian. Jagger made a beeline to the man in charge, stood at attention until he was acknowledged.

"Were in the shit here soldier," the CO said, not looking up, but clearly acknowledging Jagger.

"What just hit us, sir?" Jagger asked.

Irritated eyes looked up at him. They saw him, then they glancing over at Camila where they remained a second too long. "You tell me, son."

"They sure as hell aren't ours," Jagger spat.

A nearby explosion shook the ground, causing everyone to pause. Turning back to Jagger with a worried glance, he said, "Who are you, *soldier?*"

"First Lieutenant Jagger Justus and Second Lieutenant Camila Cardoza. Just arrived for advanced training on the Tilt-Rotors, but we're useful wherever you need us."

"Marines," he said, not any way, just...non-committal.

"Where do you need us?" Jagger said.

"Are you as good with a gun as you are with a helo?"

"We're Marines," Camila replied in response, her voice surprisingly sturdy in spite of the unfolding chaos. "We're good at everything."

Appraising her with the eyes of a man out of his depth, he nodded then said, "Let's hope to God you're right because this is way beyond FUBAR."

"Sure looks that way," Camila replied.

The day burned off and night settled in, a cool breeze gusting off the water. The drones were impossible to see in the dark, but they seemed to have retreated, for now. Reinforcements arrived and the second shift relieved the first. Rather than grabbing a hot meal and a warm bed, they were given sandwiches some of the staff made from the evacuated Subway on E. Street next to the Fitness Express and the E. Street Gym.

Jagger and Camila put a foot-long sandwich down in nothing flat, both exhausted from the fight. Bellies full, eyelids bobbing, they both grabbed fifteen minutes shut-eye against the hanger wall before heading back into the hot zone. Those fifteen minutes stretched on. Jagger simply shut his eyes; Camila leaned against him and she winked out, too.

When Jagger woke, it was to someone yelling at him to get up, that they were needed on the M249 SAW, a light belt-fed machine gun.

His eyes opened as Camila was lifting her head off his shoulder. He looked up, saw a man looking down on them, his eyes shot through with worry. Camila moved off Jagger and they both stood, groggy and heavy in the lid. Somehow they managed to sleep through the night, a surprise to them both.

"Did you hear me?" the man asked.

"Yeah," Jagger said. "We heard you."

He turned and headed out.

"When the hell did they get one of those?" she asked, referring to the M249 SAW.

Jagger shrugged his shoulders.

"I thought us sleeping together would've been more eventful than that," Camila murmured.

"Stow it, Cardoza," he grumbled, rubbing his eyes.

"They're hitting everything," Jagger heard someone telling the CO at the hub. Jagger and Camila were heading toward the guns when a young kid with a buzzed head pulled up next to them and said, "You were on the fifties yesterday, right?"

"We were," Jagger said.

"You as good on the SAW?" he asked.

"Let's hope," Jagger replied, stifling a yawn.

"I'm the runner," he said. He'd be running them the ammo belts to them.

"Don't get shot out there," Camila said.

"Try not to fall asleep," the kid replied, to which both of them gave affirmative nods.

"You okay, Lt?" Camila asked, her eyes as heavy looking as his felt.

"Peachy, you?"

"I have to admit," she said, keeping up in spite of him having six inches of height on her and longer legs, "all jokes aside, I was pretty cozy back there."

"A little too cozy for the middle of a war zone," he said.

"Says who?"

He let out a short, low laugh and said, "Shooting or feeding?"

"You shoot, I'll feed," she said with a tone. He looked at her and she gave him a suggestive wink.

"Really?" he asked.

Now out in the open where a veritable war was underway, they sprinted to the gun, and straight into the middle of hell. Behind them, their runner kept pace with the ammo belts. Turning from ill-timed seductress back to a hardened Marine, Camila grabbed the disintegrating feed strips and loaded the first belt into the feed tray.

She dropped the cover as the runner sprinted back for more ammo.

Above them, drones were everywhere. Gunfire peppered the air, air that smelled of smoke and seawater.

"You're good to go, Lt.," she said over the noise. Steadying himself, Jagger opened fire, and for the next nine hours they went to work protecting the base and each other.

By the end of the day, his arms were loose and weak and his back was a twist of painful knots. Camila said, "When we're alone tonight, I'm going to rub your back."

"Normally I'd say no," Jagger said, "but right about now, I'd let you do just about whatever you wanted. Problem is, we're not going to be alone, not in the middle of this."

When they were finally relieved of duty and they had a short travel window, the two of them boarded a bus heading off base. They crossed the JFK Memorial Causeway and pulled into a boat storage facility next to an O'Reilly auto parts store they were told was converted into makeshift barracks. The cots were lined up tight, half of them filled with snoring soldiers, maybe more.

"Grab some shut-eye, we'll come get you when we need you," they were told.

To their escort, Jagger said, "Anyone got an open line?"

"Follow me."

Jagger looked at Camila and she said, "I'll save you one."

He was led to a table serving as on-site HQ, then offered an open line. He dialed the number, waited as it rang, then heard a frantic voice on the other end.

"Jagger?"

"Hey baby, it's me."

"Oh, thank God!" Lenna said. "What's going on?"

"You heard about it?" he asked. Of course she heard about it. An attack like the one they were enduring would certainly make the news.

"Heard about it?" she asked, the line cutting in and out. "We're living it! I barely even got the boys home without getting killed!"

"Wait, what?" he asked, struggling to hear her. "Did you just say someone was killed?"

"No, Jagger," she said, the line clearing. "I said we were *almost* killed."

"How?" he asked, nearly speechless.

"They didn't tell you?" she asked. "Do you even know what's going on here?"

"No, I don't," he said. "Are Hagan and Ballard okay? Are they safe?"

"San Francisco is under attack!" she said, the line dipping and dropping off before coming back strong. "I don't know what's happening, only that the Financial District is getting bombed to smithereens!"

"Who's bombing you?" he asked, hysterical.

"Jagger?" she said.

"I'm here," he said, sticking a finger in his ear and turning away from the rows of cots filled with sleeping men and women.

"Jagger? Are you there?" she asked, the digital interference of the line drowning her voice, distorting it.

"I'm here," he said a little louder, ignoring a few wayward glances.

"I thought I lost you," she said frantic, the clarity returning. "When are you coming home? We need you here!"

"Babe, we're under attack here, too. We've been at it for the last eighteen hours. It's leveled off though. We're praying the worst is over."

"Well it isn't over for us!" she cried, the sound of fresh tears hitting her eyes before static overtook the conversation.

"Lenna?" Nothing. "Lenna!" Then the sound of an empty line. "Dammit!" he said, hanging up the phone.

"Bad reception?"

His eyes went to an old geezer behind the bank of phones. His hound dog eyes held no secrets, nor did they convey the stress of this situation. Jagger wondered if the man even understand what was happening here.

"Did you know San Francisco is under attack?" he said on a harsh whisper.

Those big, wet eyes didn't blink.

"Well?"

Making a face, rolling his jaw, he said, "So is L.A., San Diego and Sacramento if California is your concern."

"It is!"

"You didn't ask about Arizona, Texas, or Florida."

Jagger glared at him like he'd lost his mind. The geezer blinked once, twice, then dug a pinkie finger in his ear like he had no concept of the danger they might still be in. He pulled the pinkie finger out, then inspected it.

"I only asked about California because that's where my family's at," he said.

"Reports are coming in," the man offered.

"And?" Jagger all but growled.

"They're saying the drones are autonomous, that this is Armageddon."

# THE INFERNAL REGIONS: CHAPTER 2

"She's losing too much blood," I hear myself saying. Macy's shirt is red and wet. I peel it back, stare at the blood-soaked bandage. It's clear the blood is clotting, but it's not clotting fast enough. I check her pulse. It's too low.

Measuring the blood loss, suddenly concerned about her platelet count, I start to consider a blood transfusion. She's type-A, as am I, but I don't have a blood bag. Or saline. Or even drip lines or an IV needle. If she doesn't start improving, I'll have to consider her situation critical. By then it might be too late.

"Rider, you're going to Hagan's right now, yes?" I ask.

"Yes," he says.

"Do you know where a nearby hospital is?"

"No," he replies.

"I do," Hagan says, chiming in. "There's one on Cherry Street, but half of it is blown up."

"We can stop by there anyway," Rider tells me.

"How familiar are you with medical equipment and supplies?" I ask.

"Very."

"Were you in the medical field?" I ask.

"Yes, and no," he says, shifting on his feet. He looks at Indigo and she looks back, clearly out of her depth. "I'm more battle-field trained than anything."

"What's your history?" I ask, suddenly curious.

"Classified."

"Military?" I ask.

"Sure."

"So if I tell you I need a saline bag, type A blood, a drip tube and an IV needle for a blood transfusion, you'd know what to get?"

"I would. But I don't know if I'll find what you're looking for in a hospital that's half destroyed. And I can't imagine there being fresh blood on site, or even available for that matter. With the power out, refrigeration will be a thing of the past."

"We have to try."

"I can see what they have. I'm assuming you'll need clamps and a filter."

"Everything if you can," I tell him. "A stand too, if you can find one."

"What about bags?"

"Those I need for sure. Macy and I have the same blood type, so I'll be the donor if you can't find fresh blood. But you need the saline solution, too."

Just then Macy opens her eyes and says, "Mom?" She blinks twice slowly, looks up and Rider and then Indigo, then licks her dry lips. I can see she's chewing on the pain, that it's about to get worse. "I can't feel my arm."

"I know, sweetheart," I say, brushing her hair back. She's a bit warm, maybe the start of a fever. To Indigo, I say, "Do you have any Tylenol?"

"You need it now?"

"Not yet. I just need to know if you have some."

"Why can't I take it now?" Macy asks. She's bit peaked, and slightly delirious by the drunken sound of her. "Everything hurts."

"Your blood isn't clotting fast enough," I explain. "And

Tylenol is a blood thinner. So until we can get some of my blood into you, and get you clotting properly, we'll have to wait."

The concern of infection and the onset of a fever now sits front and center on my mind. I want to scream at them to go, but inside I battle to keep it together.

"I need you to go," I tell Rider. "Now. And grab everything else you can think of when you're out there."

"Will do," he says. "And good luck."

Macy's eyes are heavy. Her pulse is weak. She looks up at me, eyelids bobbing open and shut, slowly, and she says, "Am I going to die?"

Leaning down, lovingly cupping her cheek, I say, "No baby, you're going to be just fine."

But when I look up into Rider's eyes, he sees the panic, my uncertainty, and most of all a sort of desperation I know I'm failing to hide. Looking back down, I see her eyelids dipping and then she's out again.

"I'll get you what you need," Rider says, more solemn. Then to Hagan, "Let's go, kid."

When they're finally gone and I hear the Jeep's engine turn over and catch, the start of a million possible reactions to a possible blood transfusion set in.

If she has an allergic reaction to the transfusion, we're talking shortness of breath, wheezing, red welts, the flushing of her skin —or even the high-pitched sounds of stridor. It's also possible she could have an anaphylactic reaction, the signs of which are also flushing of the skin, shortness of breath and wheezing. Unique to this reaction is low blood pressure, the struggle to breathe, cramps, tightening of the chest and localized swelling.

That's my biggest concern right now.

"I can see what you're doing," Stanton says, putting a hand on my shoulder. I knew he was there, but lately he's become a bit of a wallflower. "You need to stop. You need to trust she'll be okay."

I find comfort in his face, in his steady eyes. "She's our baby,

Stanton," I say a little too loudly due to my traumatized ear drum. Stanton nods slowly, and I know he's feeling the same concern. Still, I feel better knowing he's here.

"What can I get you?" he asks.

"A cold compress. Something to lower her temperature." To Indigo, I say, "Do you have a thermometer?"

"My dad does," she says, disappearing upstairs. Rex follows her up there and I don't even want to think about him. About them. If there even is a them.

God, that's *so* not an issue right now!

Stanton returns with a wash cloth that's slightly damp and cool. I mop the sweat from her brow, place the cloth over her forehead. Her breathing changes, but she doesn't wake.

"Do you mind if I head outside and water the hole?"

"You talking about taking a pee break?" I ask.

"Yeah," Stanton says, not an ounce of humor in his eyes.

"You're fine," I say, trying to keep my voice low despite my hearing issues.

The whole idea of having no running water, meaning no toilets or functioning bathrooms, is depressing enough without all of this to contend with. My beautiful husband kisses me on top of my head, then hurries out the back door to do his business out back.

It's then that I think about my injured eardrum. I realize I heard Stanton speaking more clearly than before; he didn't sound close, but he wasn't a hollow murmur that sounded miles away either.

Regarding my ear, most of the ringing seems to have passed. There's still some pain, but it's not as much as I expected. Maybe it's not ruptured after all. I focus on it more intently. The ache isn't deep inside my ear as much as it's a sharp external stinging. This has me considering the signs of perforation, signs that aren't present: a deep and nauseous pain, loss of balance, sustained hearing loss, itching, headache.

There was blood though, wasn't there?

Turning to Atlanta, who's sitting at the kitchen table looking lost and so small in all of this, I say, "Atlanta, sweetheart, will you come have a look at my ear?"

With a weak smile, she gets up, comes over and says, "What am I looking for?"

I draw my hair back, then turn my ear toward her and say, "Just tell me what you see on the outside, first."

"Lots of little cuts," she replies. This has me breathing easier. Could the gunshot sound in my ear have traumatized the ear drum, but not perforated it?

"What does it look like?" I ask.

She takes the compress from Macy's head without asking and dabs the side of my ear and the skin around it. She shows me the cloth and all the little blood smears on it.

"So it's cut on the outside?" I ask, already knowing the answer.

Atlanta nods.

"Thank you," I say.

Smiling, she hands me the compress. I take it from her, setting the clean side back on Macy's forehead.

Before she leaves, I say, "How bad?"

The little blonde pixie leans down, draws back my hair, uses a fingernail to scratch and dig something out of the skin near my ear.

I feel whatever it is pull loose.

She shows me a tiny scrap of plaster. *Can it be?* Atlanta and I survived a hail of gunfire while tucked into a small alcove across from the school. This had to be shrapnel from that fight. Rolling the shard between my fingers, I realize this is what peppered the side of my face.

"How many little cuts?" I ask, looking up at her.

"About five. No, six. They're not that bad, though. And they're mostly around your ear."

"Thanks again," I say, my relief palpable.

All that tightness in my chest suddenly loosens. With this

new set of information, I tell myself I no longer have to worry about myself, that I should focus solely on my daughter.

"Before you sit back down," I ask, "can you bring me a tissue?"

She returns right away with one. Upstairs I hear the squeak and squeal of the wooden floor, which I know from living in the old lady's house below Gunner back in Anza Vista, are the sounds of people walking around. The way I hear drawers opening and closing, I realize the bathroom must be above us.

Rolling a square of toilet tissue into a funnel, I gently ease it into my ear canal, worrying this might cause a spike of pain but praying it doesn't. There's no pain. When I remove it, the tissue is clean and now I'm convinced my ear will be just fine.

"What are you looking for?" Atlanta asks.

"White or yellow discharge. Or blood. It indicates a perforated eardrum."

"Is that what you think happened?"

"When my hearing went, I started to panic. Then I was afraid of tinnitus—"

"What's that?"

"Phantom sounds in your ear. Like running water or what it sounds like when air escapes."

"That's part of that? Like what happens when you get a—"

"Perforated ear drum, yes," I explain, finishing the girl's sentence. "That and pain deep inside the ear canal, vertigo and sometimes nausea."

"So you're okay then?" she asks. "You have none of that?"

"I think I'll be okay," I say and watch the relief flood into her face. I suddenly understand why she's asking. She feels guilty. Like she's to blame. "This wasn't your fault, Atlanta. Even if something is wrong. Even if my ear drum had burst, that wouldn't be on you."

"I shot near your ear," she says.

"Because you had to. Do you realize if you hadn't, maybe

neither of us would be here right now? We were lucky. If not for you, and Hagan..."

Atlanta looks away, pale, perfectly still. She's still stuck on the memories of the school massacre. I don't blame her. I am, too. My heart aches for the girl, for what she's been forced to endure, for all the tragedies yet to come.

"Is she going to be alright?" Atlanta finally asks, her eyes locked on Macy.

"I don't know," I admit, taking my daughter's wrist again and counting her pulse. She'd been shot twice inside the school. She'd gone after the shooter after he'd mowed down dozens of men, women and children.

*God, what was she thinking?!*

Indigo comes down the stairs, quiet as a mouse yet wasting no time. "I couldn't find it at first," she says, handing me the thermometer.

"Thanks," I say.

I open Macy's mouth, gently slide the thermometer under her tongue, then close it again and hold her chin in place. I know I should do it rectally for a more accurate reading, but not in this environment, and not on this couch.

The reading comes back: 103.1°.

"She's running a fever," I say, dread coursing through me. I pull back the bandage on her chest, see the seeping wound, wonder again why it's not clotting. She was never a fast healer when she was young, but she never had clotting issues either.

The fear of infection settles over me and I try to calm myself. I examine her shoulder wound, see the same thing: clotting on the edges of the wound, but not nearly enough to stem the still constant flow.

"Do you have any more towels?" I ask Indigo. Rex comes down the stairs, his face weary not only from exhaustion, but from the drain of emotion.

"I do," she says. "I'll grab some water, too."

Rex sits down next to me, puts his hand on my arm and says,

"When all hell was breaking loose, she froze, so I pushed her." He doesn't say anything for a moment, then: "We were under fire, everyone in the foyer was dying, and I smacked her. I tried to shake her out of her daze. I told her to get it together."

"It's not your fault, Rex," I say, a picture of this springing to mind. "You probably saved her life."

Beside me, I feel him swipe away a tear. Looking up, seeing his damp eyes, I say, "She's going to be okay. She'll pull through."

"Do you really believe that?" he asks, another tear rolling off his eyelid and drifting down his cheek.

"If I didn't, then I wouldn't be able to do this."

"What if we don't find the blood, and you can't do a transfusion?" he asks, the concern laid bare in his eyes. "What then?"

I can't bring myself to say it, because that's the fear that's chewing at my insides, my sanity, everything solid and stable within me.

"She'll be fine, Rex."

The sad thing is, he's looking at me knowing I don't really believe this. Deep down, I realize I'm preparing myself for the worst, for the honest-to-God notion that I just might lose my little girl.

# YOUR VOICE MATTERS

Emerging authors like me still get that writer's high reading the great reviews from readers like yourself, but there's more to a review than an author's personal gratification. As independent writers, we don't have the financial might of New York's Big 5 publishing firms, and we'd never shell out a gazillion dollars to Barnes & Noble for that ultra-prime shelf space (*yet!*). What we *do* have, however, is far more valuable than shelf space or movie contracts or all the marketing money in the world: we have you, *the devoted reader.* If you enjoyed this book, I'd be immensely grateful if you could leave a quick and easy review on the Amazon page where you bought the book or at the link below. Not only do reviews like yours help this series get the exposure it needs to grow and thrive, reading your kind reviews has become the highlight of my day, so please be sure to leave a word or two if you can.

*\*Please note, the way Amazon's review system works is five stars is good, four stars is alright, and three stars or less is just degrees of no bueno. Thanks again!*

To leave a review, simply type in **amazon.com/author/ryan-**

**schow** then select the book you're reviewing, then scroll down about half the page to the review section and tap the bar that says: WRITE A CUSTOMER REVIEW, and you're good!

To join the invitation-only (you're invited!) Facebook fan page, simply type in THE LAST WAR FAN GROUP in the Facebook browser (search bar) and join our ever growing community!